Ten Fa

Abi Titmuss

with

Jayne Lockwood

First published in 2005 by
Virgin Books
Thames Wharf Studios
Rainville Road
London W6 9HA

A catalogue record for this book is available from the British Library.

ISBN 0 7535 10375

Design and typesetting by Phoenix Photosetting, Chatham, Kent
Printed and bound in Great Britain by William Clowes Ltd, Beccles, Suffolk

Contents

# *Acknowledgments*

Thanks to Emma Rouse and Francis Ridley at Money.

Also thank you to my bunnies – Mick, Sue and DD – this is dedicated to you girls.

Introduction

My first words are to thank you for buying my book. I hope that you enjoy reading it as much as I enjoyed creating it. You probably know a little bit about me but, although you may have seen many images of me, you won't have seen into my mind – which, like most women, is where I get really racy.

I've always had a strong imagination when it comes to sex, and I really enjoyed letting it run wild with this book. I even surprised myself when writing the really hot bits and had to take a 'break' at times! Maybe you will feel the same reading them. Many of us skip to the naughty bits in a sexy novel, so that's why I chose to write ten short stories that you can dip in and out of easily when the mood takes you.

Like most women I love sexy books and I still remember the first Black Lace book I read as a teenager. In fact, I still have it! It is called *No Paradise But Pleasure*, and came free with a copy of a women's magazine.

I've always been a bit naughty and, from the age of sixteen, I realised I had a high sex drive, which definitely seems to be getting stronger as I get older. Looking back, the kind of men that first sparked my arousal tended to be – sorry to sound clichéd – working guys like builders. I remember one guy in particular who was working on a house near where I lived. I was seventeen. He must have been about twenty-two – blond, tanned, muscular and gorgeous in the sun as he hammered and sawed in ripped jeans and no top. I would spot him as I made my way home from school. Summer was underway, and when I passed him I would pull my school skirt up so it looked shorter than it really was. Everyday I knew he would be looking for me to walk past at 4p.m. and I would pause and hold his gaze for a few seconds. He would stare right back at me, all sweaty and dusty and then give a little smile that said, 'I know exactly what you want.' I was thrilled by his interest in me and it made my stomach flip. On the days I saw him I'd then go home and think about him at night, nourishing my new-found sexual imagination and inventing scenarios where things would go further than 'just looking'. Since then I can't deny I've always had a thing for, for want of a better phrase, 'a bit of rough'. I'm sure many women share this feeling with me. I know most men have a similar thing for nurses and I can see why.

When I was a student nurse at university I had a crush on a Sister on the ward I worked on. She looked so strong and sexy in her navy-blue Sister's uniform and her shiny dark hair pinned up. I couldn't take my eyes off her. Then, of course, there were the doctors in their white coats; not to mention some of the sexy young male patients I looked after – but I don't want to give too much away!

One of things I love about being a woman – and it's why books of fantasies work for us girls – is that we can be turned on just by using our minds, without anything having to physically happen. One of the sexiest events my life was actually incredibly simple. One day, before I was famous, and just another girl in London, I was rushing through the City trying to find a black cab. It was a baking summer's day and I was wearing a very thin blouse, a short pleated skirt and strappy summer sandals. Suddenly there was a storm and sheets of heavy warm rain began to fall. It was the kind of shower you experience on the continent – sudden, short-lived and completely drenching – where if you don't have an umbrella you urgently have to find somewhere to shelter. I was caught right in it.

After the relentless sticky heat of the City I was longing to get home, rip my clothes off and stand under a cool shower. As I ran looking for cover I was actually enjoying the feel of the rain on my face and against my skin. However, within a couple of minutes, my hair was plastered to my head and I could feel my mascara stinging as the water trickled into my eyes. My legs were wet and shiny and my feet slipped around in my sandals. Every doorway and bus shelter was full of people in suits, patiently waiting out the storm. It made me smile to notice how, during moments like that, forced together and wet, people in London will make the effort to acknowledge each other and their predicament and exchange a few self-conscious words before the rain stops and they step out again, eyes fixed either on the pavement or straight ahead as they ignore one another again.

I eventually spotted a concealed doorway to an old London bank which no one had noticed and I practically threw myself into it, laughing to myself at just how wet I was. It was a little gloomy and I leaned back against the cool stone wall, rain dripping off my ears and the end of my nose. I wiped my eyes and was just running my hands through my wet hair when someone burst into my hideaway, laughing to himself just as I had. We both gasped, equally surprised to see each other, and then we smiled awkwardly. My initial annoyance at the intrusion into my little space quickly turned to curiosity. As he quickly put down his briefcase and leaned back against the wall opposite I looked him up and down. He was quite a bit older than me, maybe in his forties, dressed immaculately in a well-cut modern suit and crisp white shirt, open at the neck with no tie.

His body was perfectly in proportion – tall and broad-shouldered – and his hands were beautiful, clean and masculine. As my gaze moved up his body I realised my heartbeat quickened and I wasn't sure why. His neck glistened with rain and a drop of water trickled down his cheek into his open shirt neck. As I took in his strong jaw line I almost jumped with the realisation that he was looking at me, too, and doing exactly to me what I was doing to him. I became acutely aware of my body. I was wet through in my thin summer clothes, and I might as well have been standing in front of him naked. I glanced down at my blouse and saw that it was virtually transparent and stuck to my skin. The white bra I had on underneath was sheer and both it and my nipples were clearly visible. Even writing this now recaptures how breathless I felt.

As our eyes met it was like an electric charge went through my body. I looked away and suddenly felt embarrassed, thinking to myself that I must look awful – soaking wet hair, make–up running etc. He looked barely dishevelled and so handsome in comparison but I could feel him still looking at me. My pulse was racing and I could feel my nipples were hard and betraying me through my wet blouse. I looked at him again. We stood there, two complete strangers hiding from the rain and everyone else, soaking wet and staring at each other. I felt small, young and powerless, without my hair and make-up and with my clothes so transparent.

My overwhelming emotion was that I wanted to seduce him. Urgently. And the force of my aroused state shocked me. I think there must be something very powerful in the energy of a storm, as it can trigger passionate or irrational behaviour. I somehow felt I could blame the wild weather for that sudden surge in my libido. As I held his gaze, I was so turned on and willing him to take just one step forward, push me against the cold wall and really kiss me.

The rain went on and on and we continued to look at

each other, enjoying the incredible tension of this chance meeting. Then he spoke. I don't remember what he said but it was small talk and I responded. We talked a little more, only a few stilted words, and I was praying for the rain not to stop so the moment would last a little longer. Sadly I could see it was drying up and I already knew that I was never going to see this man again. After all, we didn't even know each other's names and, although I wanted to know his, the anonymity made it more exciting. The rain all but stopped and we both reluctantly stepped out of our secret space. Where the shower had been so heavy it had felt almost like a curtain across the doorway through which no one could see, and now we were on the other side of it again. Back in the throng of the City ... and reality.

We looked at each other and, breathing a little heavily, said goodbye, then turned slowly and walked in opposite directions. After a few paces I just had to look back at him and my stomach flipped as he did exactly the same. I smiled, turned and carried on home. To this day I remember so clearly how I felt that afternoon – and shortly after it happened I was driven crazy that I didn't seduce him! I tortured myself with the 'what if?' and I can't help wondering now if he knows what he missed. But, on the same note, it was perfect as it was.

The 'what if?' factor is something we all daydream about when it comes to meeting fanciable strangers. You sit opposite someone on a train journey, pass them on an escalator, are drawn to them across a bar or hold a gaze at a concert, and your mind can take you off in flights of fancy. This book is a collection of my personal, uncensored 'what ifs?'. They range from the impressionistic to the down and dirty, but all of them are exciting and all of them come straight from my mind. I'll leave you to guess which of them may really have happened.

I believe that sexual freedom and expression is good for us and, with the busy stressful lives we all lead these days, it's very important to take time out for a little pleasure. So relax and enjoy my fantasies. Whether you read them all in one sitting or dip in when you have a moment to yourself, I hope there' s something in here you really like.

Abi, April 2005

I

Who's the Boss?

I stand in the shower for a long time. Hot needles of water beat against my skin. Warm my blood. Relax me. When I'm done I step out into clouds of steam, jasmine fragrant. Luxury first thing in the morning – I need it. Breakfast ... what shall I have? Fresh-ground coffee, bagels baked earlier that morning from the deli across the street, plum conserve from Fortnum & Mason. Slinking into a robe of Egyptian cotton, I go down to the kitchen and eat.

After I've devoured my continental breakfast I spend a long time smoothing Molton Brown moisturiser into my skin, and blow-drying my hair until it is soft and shiny before tying it up and away from my face in a businesslike chignon. Underwear next – my secret weapon. I want a glossy second skin to enhance my assets; see-through but with the sheen of polished glass under bedroom lights. Naughty but chic. A bra that whispers erotic allure with its sheer pink cups. Matching transparent knickers with a cheeky satin bow at the back. And then it has to be stockings. Nothing else will do. Fine black nylon that I roll up my legs before clipping the shiny tops to black suspenders with silver clips. Wearing such outrageously sexy lingerie under my sober work clothes is sure to give me a secret thrill as I sit among the dry and serious men I will try to prise money out of.

One part of my wardrobe is home to a variety of take-no-prisoners business clothes, and today I choose a suit. Formal but feminine. So much is riding on this meeting and I have to get the uniform just right. Disarm my opponents. Win an early advantage. But anything too severe and it will look like I'm trying too hard; like an office junior at her first interview. I need a balance between the sexy and the formal.

I choose a thin white cotton blouse – cool and sophisticated and tight around my bust. Then the jacket ... which is black with wide, sharp lapels and a nipped-in waist. The skirt has a snug fit, hard lines and rides an inch above my knees. I bought the suit in New York, and it shows: tailored simplicity and guaranteed to create an impression wherever it goes. Shoes follow, not too high, but with pointed toes and elegant heels to show off my ankles to their best advantage. I am dressed for battle with an enemy that will be surprised by charm. Looking at my reflection, I even shiver slightly. A spritz of Issey Miyake perfume calms me, helps me to focus. My manicured fingernails curl around the black Gucci briefcase and I'm ready.

I'll soon be chairing a meeting – a very important one. One that will decide whether the company I am director of – let's call it Inca Solutions – will expand to become a leader in its field, or remain a sturdy but unremarkable name on the periphery. Since taking over as chief executive a year before, my goal is to thrust Inca into the premier league and ensure it stays there. Only, I have one little problem ...

Finances. I need them. But have a lucrative proposition in my sights. And have made progress with a group of curious investors who see Inca as a viable proposition. But there is a serious flaw in my plans – certain men who find it difficult to take me and my proposals seriously. Particular men who work for the accountancy firm I inherited from the previous

CEO of my company, and led by an old-school number cruncher, reluctant to take risks. And he will be there today, to pour cold water on any enthusiasm and promise of a deal.

The offices of Inca Solutions are near the river. From my office I can see the London Eye and the building affectionately known as the 'erotic gherkin' in the distance. As views go, it's exceptional. Not bad on the inside, either. I have decked out my office in calming cream with chocolate-brown trimmings. It is understated and tasteful, exclusive but not ostentatious. Outside my door, the rest of our firm's interior is designed with similar restraint and class. The staff have their own workstations because I don't believe in hot-desking like the previous management. As a result, morale has risen and so have the figures in the accounts books. Good numbers, but not good enough. Not yet.

I greet my assistant, Janey, who hands over my messages and post. I call Inca's accountant, Luke, to come into my office so we can discuss strategy for the meeting, scheduled to begin in less than an hour.

There are six of us in the boardroom: Luke and I, plus the two investors and two representatives from Coles, our accountants. I have arranged to have the investors seated at the window end of the large boardroom table. A ploy. It is the investors' first visit to Inca's offices and I want them to take in the length and glossiness of the table, to admire the splendid view and be convinced this is a company of weight and stature. An outfit deserving investment.

OK, so I'm desperate for their money. I'd consider anything – even sleeping with their chief if I thought it would help. But when I see him – squat, bald, 55 – I change my mind. With the best will in the world, a pass will never look convincing.

The accountants from Coles wear matching no-nonsense expressions. Arthur Walpole, the eldest, I'm used to. He berates me on occasion about the size of my expense account, totally oblivious to the importance of Manolos in a successful executive's career. The younger one, James, doesn't look much fun, either, although he is one hell of a lot easier on the eye. Short, straight black hair, narrow Hugo Boss spectacles, and a dark suit that looks like a Ted Baker. His cuffs are snow white, surrounding slim wrists dusted with silky hair, and a heavy silver wristwatch, obviously expensive, but not, I am pleased to note, a Rolex. All his accessories, from the slim camel attaché case to the discreet cufflinks that flash a little colour, suggest style with restraint. Earlier he shook my hand with a firm grip and looked at me with eyes so blue they could have been stolen from an arctic sea. A faint aroma of Calvin Klein aftershave tantalised my nostrils and I felt a shiver of lust. This was a man I would like to get to know.

However, he is no flirt, and his manner is brisk. If I think I am going to get around him by batting my eyelashes, I am very much mistaken. My subtle signals – the brush of legs under the table, the gentle hand on the wrist or on the back – go unrequited. He won't notice me! It is very frustrating.

Janey and another girl come in with fragrant coffee and dainty beignets that vanish after a couple of nips. I learned early in my career that doughnuts don't go down well; the constant wiping away of sugar and jam interferes with serious discussion.

The meeting confirms my expectations: the investors are interested, but our accountants keep throwing tax-law anvils to flatten their enthusiasm. If I think Arthur is old school, I am totally unprepared for James. He is hardcore. Emotionless, steady, straight-backed; a rock I want to crack. I clench my teeth under a professional smile. Now I want to shake him. No, not shake, but slam him over the boardroom table and rip his clothes off. That's what I want to do. What I need to do.

I find him very distracting. So serious and professional,

with a submerged sense of dry humour lying so deep it may not actually even exist. Yet all the same I want him. He's so unreadable. It's why I want him. How dare he resist me? I restrain myself from making overt gestures in order to get his attention. Is the man a celibate, or does he have a heavy relationship going with some lucky girl and simply isn't interested? I'm desperate to know, but the talk is strictly business and I have to stay focused on the back-and-forth across the table if I want these investors on board. The accountants are still doing their best to sabotage the idea and, again, I am surprised at James. For such a good-looking, intense man he seems curiously staid when it comes to risk. What is it with this guy? Does he not have any edge?

Finally, after lunch at the local steakhouse, I get a moment alone with him and begin my subtle interrogation. The investors have left, saying they will call me the following day. Arthur has drifted off to another client meeting and Luke is working on last year's accounts. I hold James back with some phony questions about corporate tax, as he is an expert. Of course, he couldn't say no. And we need to be alone, away from the clatter of plates and cutlery, so we can really get down to business.

So I take him back to the boardroom, give him coffee, and after a few trivial questions about tax allowances I ask him a probing question. What is his problem with taking risks? Doesn't he agree we have to move on?

'Of course, but we have to work within the parameters of acceptable risk, as well as the law,' he says stubbornly.

'I'm aware of that.' My tone is sharp. I try to soften it. 'That wasn't the kind of risk I was referring to. My company ...'

'Is successful in its own right,' he chips in. 'If what you're proposing goes belly up, Inca's reputation might be damaged for good. If you do survive, it'll take a long time to win back your good name. People don't like failure.'

'Oh please! Don't patronise me with that speech,' I suddenly blurt out, my passions finding a new channel. 'I heard it in business college eight years ago.' I pace in front of the window, frustrated with him. How can I convince this man to take a risk? I doubt he's ever taken one in his life. I spin round and look him in the eye.

'What's the most daring thing you've ever done?' I ask, leaning in slightly closer – enough for him to catch a zephyr of my perfume.

That startles him; I see the shock at my impertinence register around those astonishing blue eyes. But they soon narrow and the way he looks at me changes. Becomes more intense. One eyebrow rises, ever so slightly. I detect his displeasure with me; an anger not at all unattractive. And fighting against this is the professional discipline, the code of business – no raised voices or strong emotion to be betrayed by the even features of his handsome face. He considers my question for a moment, then says in a calm, straight voice, 'You really want to know?'

'Enlighten me. Impress me,' I say, goading, provoking him; wanting to bring that lovely shadow back into his eyes.

'When I was eighteen and thought I knew it all, I wanted to impress my girlfriend by being a big shot trader. From my bedroom I was going to perform a miracle and make a killing. Then ask the girl to marry me after buying her a diamond ring. So I set up a dummy company. Put in a phone-line. My parents thought it was a university project. Business studies. I dropped my Dad's name to gain credibility. He was a well known fund manager at the time. You could say, looking after other people's money is in my blood. So, wearing my Dad's red braces over a silly chalk-stripe shirt, I borrowed forty grand from some investors. Did it all over the phone. Then invested it in African minerals on a tip from another idiot my own age. Two months before a civil war kicked off in that country. Forty grand of stock became lots of zeros with nothing in front of the decimal point, in a heartbeat. So I borrowed another ten and made a wild stab into pharmaceuticals, which made a profit of thirty five after clearing the initial stake. Still leaving me five grand in the red overall. I lost eight kilos and didn't see daylight for two weeks. But I got off lightly – the five I owed could have been fifty. Though I still had to take that long walk down to my dad's study and ask for five grand to pay off my bad investments.'

'That's better!' I nod with approval and flash him a cheeky smile. 'What did he do to you?'

'Sold my car and got me a job in a supermarket, stacking shelves all night for three months. At the weekends I put in twenty hours as a labourer for a builder. Didn't have a day off for the entire summer break.'

'You still with the girlfriend?' I ask, smiling.

'No. She never did get that ring.'

'And I guess the bedroom office at your parent's house was shut down.'

'I have an apartment in Highgate, thanks very much.'

'Oh, so now you have the risk of a mortgage?'

The smouldering black look is back. James glances at his watch. 'I think my time here is over. I need to be back at the office.' He stands up and pushes his chair back under the table.

Stay right where you are, mate, I think: the mental image of this indifferent man sprawled over the boardroom table will not go away.

'What would happen if you didn't go back?' I ask. 'Would they fire you?'

Pausing, he looks at me. Frowns in puzzlement. 'No.

'I'm prepared to take a risk,' I say, walking towards him, a playful smile in my eyes.

'But...' He looks at the door, then at me.

Holding his stare, I reach out and run one of my buffed and shining nails over a nipple concealed beneath the crisp cotton of his tailored shirt. I'm very good at targeting a man's erogenous zones, and James's reaction tells me I've hit the spot – his lips part, his eyes go a little dreamy, his cheeks flush.

'Was there another kind of risk you wanted to discuss?' he whispers, his voice hoarse.

I pick up his right hand and slip it inside my jacket, over my breast, and hold it there. His fingers are unyielding, unsure and fail to curve around the soft opportunity that has fallen into the palm of his hand. An opportunity so plentiful, it even spills over the sides.

He breathes hard. Pupils widen. Against my hand his heart beat starts a drum solo. My own nipples tighten to the warmth and pressure of his long fingers, and my breasts swell with arousal. When I let go of his wrist he removes the hand, but not immediately. Even so, I still have to admire his self-discipline – I find it phenomenal.

'I'm finding out whether you're prepared to take the same risks as me,' I say. Though smaller than James, even in my heels, I still manage to trap him against the desk as my hand moves down towards his waistband. His eyes follow the inexorable passage of my fingers but, just before they make contact, he catches my wrist.

'No,' he says.

'Why not?' My frustration has changed to full-blown arousal, and he just isn't going to get away. He doesn't know quite what he's in for. Using my other hand, I cup his crotch and gently massage it. Something sturdy pushes back at my fingers.

'God,' he says, and leans back against the table for support. 'No. I ... don't ...'

'Don't what? Don't stop?'

Flushed and baffled, he can't look at me. 'This isn't ... ethical,' he says. His words slur, as if he has been drinking.

I move away from him, to the fat leather executive chair at the end of the table. Smiling, I open my briefcase. I withdraw a tube and a lighter. Inside the tube is a tightly rolled cigar, imported all the way from Havana. If I'm ever feeling roused by success, or I want to surprise and excite a guy, I light up a cigar. It never fails. Especially when it's combined with the business suit. Victory over this uptight man is in sight. I have unnerved him, gotten inside his head and right under his suit. His eyes are fixed on me as I take my time to light the cigar. He shivers as I draw in the first fragrant mouthful and then let it drift in a coil from my lips. He runs his fingers through his hair, mussing it up. Licks his full, boyish lips. I offer the cigar to him. 'You want some?'

Transfixed, he shakes his head. I blow a smoke ring in his direction.

'This is for real,' I say. 'I'm the boss. This is my office, my boardroom. My chair.' I squeeze the squashy leather arms of the chair, making them squeak in the silence. 'I decide what happens here.' I let my fingers fall into my lap and start gathering up my skirt. James swallows, is hypnotised by the fingers gradually revealing my stockinged legs. I raise the hem above the suspender clips, affording him a tantalising view of pale skin contrasting with shimmering nylon. 'So nobody can tell me what isn't ethical.'

Just as he is about to move towards me I flip my skirt back down again and stand up. Move close. Reach out and remove his glasses. Without them his expression is naked, vulnerable; he blinks, but that might be the shock of what is happening to him. He stands like a statue – rigid, sculpted. I take advantage and reach for the buttons on his white cotton shirt. They yield easily, allowing me to bare a broad, solidly muscled chest, cut from many hours in the gym. This man is a catch. Why has no woman snapped him up? Not for want of trying, I bet. I flick my tongue over one nipple and hear his soft intake of breath. Standing close, I slip one leg around him. His suit trousers chafe against the tender skin above my stocking top. He must be able to feel my heat through the thin knickers. I resist the temptation to rub against his thigh like a horny cat. Instead I drop my hand to his crotch. He is so hard now, his body betraying his every thought. As my hand curves around him, he stares into my eyes, as if unable to comprehend this is actually happening.

'This is an unusual way of doing business,' he says, as my tongue trails up his throat. His voice is as stiff as his erection, but he doesn't stop me unzipping his fly. Immediately, his penis pushes out, tenting the tight Lycra in his black Calvin Klein shorts. His body shudders against me as I trace a finger around the thick circumference.

'You could walk away,' I say. 'Your company doesn't need our business. You could just go back to Mr Cole and say you no longer want to work on this project.' All the time, my fingers are walking, gently, up and down his shaft. 'You could even say we were too risky. Hot headed. Too passionate about rolling the dice.' While I talk, I peel his briefs down to expose him to the warm air of the boardroom. Then I dip my head and lick him, catching him unawares. I can smell Eternity for Men, with an undertone of natural male musk. This time his gasp is audible, and ends on a strangled note when I close my lips over him completely.

'Why are you doing this?' he asks hoarsely.

I stand up again. 'Because I believe in taking risks, and I think you should learn to take a few, too. It's called living. Nothing to do with business.' I smile at him. 'And you do look damned fine in that suit.'

'So why are you doing your damnedest to take it off me?' He smiles for the first time.

'Do you really need me to answer that question?' I move in again and loosen his tie. This time he does not protest, but steadies himself against the boardroom table with his hands and allows me to unbutton, unzip, and then lick him from shaft to throat and back again. He trembles, gasps, his body moving in rhythm with mine.

'Please,' he murmurs. Then mutters something that sounds like 'more'. His head falls back and his hips begin to gyrate as he completely surrenders to me, incanting 'more' as if he's afraid I might stop pleasuring him. I suspect he is about to lose it right there, but then I feel his hand on my hair. Tenderly, he pulls me upright. Loosens my chignon, lets my locks swing free. Pushes my jacket off my shoulders. Captivated by his soft touch, I let it fall to the floor. I hold my breath as his fingers drift down my face, my throat, sending tingling messages down my body to my toes. Using both hands, he caresses me. Strong fingers smooth the silky lapels of my blouse, then loiter in the valley between my breasts. Thumbs stroke their generous swell.

Suddenly he wrenches the blouse apart. Buttons ping in every direction. The shock leaves me breathless, but no less affected than he is at the sight of my bra – and what lies inside their silky cups. His eyes fix on my nipples, now hard beneath the pinky smoke of the sheer cups. The sight of them is untying the leash of the latent animal imprisoned inside him.

Spun around, I am then spread across the table. My skirt is pushed up to my waist. He knocks my ankles apart and runs his hands over my buttocks, squeezing them roughly. The bow at the back of my knickers is only appreciated for a second before being torn loose more than untied. Then it's my turn to gasp when a lascivious tongue thrusts between my buttocks, and traces the crevice to the top. Before this exquisite sensation fully registers, my knickers are pulled down to my knees, and I am hoisted aloft by the grip of strong hands on my hips, and then spread across the table.

I roll on to my back and watch him kick off his shoes. He clambers on to the table and kneels over me. He pauses to let his eyes feast on the banquet that is my curvaceous and beautifully presented body – still fully dressed, yet obscenely exposed – before he runs his hands over my curves. These paws are hot. They tremble. Are greedy and they grasp as if not knowing what to touch first. His warm lips squash against my mouth; he tries to devour me. When his passion is answered by my tongue, lashing deep inside his mouth, he stops as if he has been slapped.

'What am I doing?' he asks, suddenly horrified.

'What does it look like?' I pull him down for a deep, thrusting kiss, and feel his body press hard against mine. Giving in to his basest desires, he gathers up my lower body, positions himself and then slams into me with a force that leaves us both wordless. Unable to stop himself, he is now driven by sheer primeval need. The expensive suit, the gold cuff links, the heavy watch are all meaningless trinkets for a man who needs nothing but a sexy woman and a flat surface to rut on.

Only once does he stop and look down at me and in his eyes I can see a reflection of my own hunger and need. 'Come on,' I whisper, and wrap my stocking-clad legs around his waist. 'I want it.'

Reason, restraint and logic are switched off in his brain. Dimly I wonder whether anyone outside can hear us as we slither and bump away on the boardroom table, knocking over glasses of Perrier, scattering copies of my business plan to the floor. My feet scrabble for purchase on the slippery surface, find it, and I give back what he is giving me. Digging my fingers into his buttocks, I feel a muscular pumping underneath my palms.

'Oh fuck, fuck, fuck,' he groans as he pulls away. I feel a warm splash across my stomach, breasts and even my neck. His breath is hot against my cheek as he wrings himself dry, before massaging his cream into my flesh.

He sits back on his heels, his head thrown back. He reminds me of a wolf about to howl. His eyes are closed, and his erection still appears firm. Finally he peers down at me. 'Who's the boss now?' he whispers, a gleam of triumph in his eyes.

I can't answer. Am still highly aroused, with the threat of frustration hanging over me like a black sky. Is he just going to walk away and leave me lying there covered in the fruits of his labour? I am crying out for release but I will not beg. That isn't my style.

He is sitting in the deep leather chair at the end of the table. My chair. Sitting there in an arrogantly spread pose, unashamed of the contented thickness dozing in the lap of his tailored trousers. It hasn't even had the decency to wilt after I had wrung him dry.

'You haven't answered my question,' he says. 'If you answer correctly, you might get what you want.'

I can't believe the man's audacity. Sparking with anger, I sit up, with as much dignity as I can manage.

'Go screw yourself,' I say. Leaning forwards, he takes my chin and forces me to look him in the eye.

'Who's the boss now?' he repeats.

I find myself slipping, responding to his game. Renewed excitement electrifies my body. If he wants to think he has power over me, I will let him kid himself to get what I want.

'You are,' I say sweetly.

James smiles. Kisses my neck. His tongue slides down, down towards my breasts. Wantonly I arch my back, exposing my nipples to his eager mouth. That tug of stubbly lips against my erect flesh reminds me I am still desperately turned on. So I lie back on the table, luxuriously stretching out as he repositions himself in the big fat leather chair. Like a lion with a fresh kill, he spreads me wide and begins to feast. Tongue long and probing, I am sent soaring on a wave of pleasure. Lapped and licked and kissed and pressed in all the right places, I bite my fingers and go to a dizzy, crazy place.

Wild-faced, his lips draw back from his teeth in a savage grimace of lust.

That night, I am just lighting the candles on the smoked glass of my dining-room table when the doorbell rings.

We enjoy a meal of antipasto, fresh pasta with wild boar ragout from *Carluccios* and a crisp Caesar salad – though I draw the line at tiramisu and instead put cheese on the table, with plump red grapes and coriander-spiced crackers. I feed him well, and ply him with Pinot Noir before leading him to my large goose-down-covered bed.

'Glad you took the risk?' I ask James as we lie among rumpled and damp Egyptian cotton sheets.

'Of course,' he says, lacing his fingers around mine. He pushes me back on the bed and begins to kiss me. I can feel him swelling against my thigh. The man is now addicted, captivated and unstoppable. 'This does put me in a very awkward position, though. Ethically, I shouldn't be sleeping with one of my clients.'

'How about unethically?'

'The world is my oyster,' he replies, and buries his face between my legs.

As I begin to relax into pleasure he pauses, looks up, smiles. 'No one has to know about this, but they might find out. If they do, it could be very awkward for you.'

Instinctively, I know he isn't saying this out of concern for me. I noticed an avaricious look in his eyes the moment he stepped into my apartment and saw the expensive furnishings and state-of-the-art kitchen equipment. A shame he has turned out to be so predictable. But then he does have a history of getting caught with his fingers in the till.

'So what are you proposing?'

'Fifteen per cent of future profits, and I'll keep my mouth shut about all those other little expenses you keep running up on the company credit. You see, after our meeting today, I have taken a much closer interest in you. Did some research back at the office, you could say. And found some interesting things none of us had seen before.' He licks me again, flickering the tip of his tongue so delicately against my bud that I can't argue with him. Instead, I smile and tease my nipples with my fingertips until they stiffen into peaks. I have turned this man into a shark, and now he is trying to devour me.

'Spend the weekend with me, and I'll make it twenty,' I say. I am taking a gamble, a *risk*, but I have another trick up my sleeve. If he wants to play dirty, so be it.

He licks me, long and slow, and looks up again. 'You really do know how to do business,' he says. Then he stops toying with me and sets to work.

I peak sooner than I expected, charged up by the thought of spending a whole weekend in the company of a sexual predator who has no idea he is dealing with a carnivore several levels above him on the food chain.

The next night my answer is ready. I feel elated for two reasons: that afternoon the investors let me know they are interested in putting a contract on the table; and the risk I had taken the night before has developed an interesting twist.

Earlier that day I had gone down to the basement of the office building. The security staff were there, sitting in front of their monitors. I talked to one of them, and we went into a private office. For a viewing on a spare screen used for playing back tapes.

And there I was in all my glory, being taken hard by my accountant on the boardroom table. Even watching it in that tiny little office in black-and-white had an instant warming effect on my libido. I took the tape away, amused at the way the security guard were unable to look me in the eye. I imagine the fun they must have had, watching the show. And they will still be thinking about it that night, and a fair few after, and the thought turns me on even more. Shameless maybe, but I didn't get this far by being a shrinking wallflower and a prude.

And now, pressing all of my buttons, is the power I can wield over James. Arthur Cole will not be impressed with his star employee seducing one of their long-standing clients. And with extortion added to the list of misdemeanours, my arm twisting can become a chokehold. Of course, I've had the video edited a little. No one will ever know it was me who did the seducing. That is between me and James. I made him hungry, greedy, insatiable. Right now he can't get enough of me, so every time he asks, 'Who's the boss?' I smile and say, 'Who do you think, darling?'

Designer Service

It's been a good year for one of London's up-and-coming stockbroking firms. An exceptional year, in fact, and the directors, as well as the accountants who have been advising them all year, are in high spirits – we can tell by the rich laughter coming through the solid oak doors of the club as they look around the hallway and take in the luxurious surroundings. The building is Georgian – and reeks of old money and fine leather, with spacious rooms decorated to appeal to men of the world. There are the low-lit reading rooms with highly polished green Chesterfield armchairs, where silent waiting staff in immaculate uniforms take discreet orders and serve drinks with old-fashioned manners. There are grand function rooms, an imposing boardroom – and bathrooms with accessories by Trumper's and other upscale men's toiletries from Jermyn Street. But my favourite room has to be the ballroom. I imagine it was used for 18th century parties, when ladies would trade secrets behind their fans and decadent gentlemen would invite them onto the polished wooden floor to dance the Waltz and the Polka. I like to think we are continuing a tradition, of entertaining men of the commercial world, beguiling them with fine wines and plying them with sumptuous feats – and picking up a few rewards of our own in the process.

The notice on the double doors of the dining room where we are holding the function says CLOSED FOR PRIVATE PARTY. The room is the most intimate of the building. The walls are a deep, dark red, adding to the air of decadent luxury, although in Georgian times they were probably duck-egg blue or a pale mint green. A long table dominates the room, covered with a crisp, white linen cloth that sweeps down to the floor. On it is set the highly polished silver cutlery and sparkling glasses for each wine course. This huge table has an elaborate centrepiece of candles in the middle, reflected on both sides by two gilt wall-length mirrors that are as grand as the windows that overlook Pall Mall.

'This should be a breeze,' Michaela, my close friend and colleague, murmurs in my ear as we check out the City boys coming up the stairs to see who we think is the fittest, the shyest, the richest, the funniest. The party is small, no more than eleven good-humoured men in black tie, more than ready to be waited on by two luscious, glossy and groomed young women like us.

'Assume the position, girl,' Michaela jokes as we dart into the kitchen to smooth the tiny white aprons over our short black skirts and check the bows on our white jersey tops for the last time. They are laced at the front and, depending on the bra worn underneath, I can look as innocent as a choirgirl or as raunchy as a serving wench. I like to be somewhere in between, depending on who I'm serving. Tonight it's a thrusting, testosterone-charged group, so I've chosen a very pretty black bra with sprigs of roses on it, which just shows through the snug white top. It uplifts my breasts just enough to provide a glimpse of cleavage every time the laces give a little. Watching professional men trying to cop a sneaky eyeful is one of my favourite pastimes when I'm working. I also have on matching panties in translucent silk with a hint of lace around the legs and a pink bow at the back; and stockings, because there isn't anything quite as thrilling as accidentally brushing against a man and watching the quizzical expression in his eyes. Is she or isn't she? And the knowledge that it would be so easy to slip his hand up my skirt and find out, without anybody knowing, as long as he didn't think I would scream and slap his face.

Which, of course, I wouldn't, unless he was really gross, but men can be so dense. In these days of political correctness, unless you write 'Please feel free to feel me up' in lipstick on their napkin, it isn't going to happen. I've never felt quite that courageous. So instead I feed their desire with Montrachet and 1962 Hennessy and hope they remember to tip me well.

Michaela's smoky eyes and full red lips say it all. She has small, high breasts and a generously sized bottom, thanks to her Brazilian roots. Long legs, shiny blonde hair for me and glossy brown for her ... between us we have all bases covered. All we have to do is convince our guests to part with as much cash as possible, and that will be my next Caribbean holiday half paid for. Michaela and I have a side of the table each. Because the party is small, the other waitresses have been dismissed for the night and we have an unspoken agreement that we are going to get up to tricks with these boys. Although nothing has been said, I know we have been chosen because we are more skilled at tempting our guests to indulge more than they would otherwise do. Fine wine, expensive liqueurs ... it all seems to make sense when looking into the succulent cleavages of doe-eyed girls who want only to please and thrill.

As we go to stand by the entrance like sentries in patent black stilettos, a swarm of dinner suits moves towards us in a cloud of Eternity and Etienne Aigner, the front four strutting like fighter pilots. Smug smiles, strong chins, good cheekbones. They give our cleavages flickering, almost contemptuous glances as we greet them. We smile back, innocent as kittens. You think you're in control, big shot, I say to myself. Wrong. So, so wrong.

And here he is, the big *kahuna*, passing us with barely a glance to take his place. The suit is subtly better quality, probably bespoke, like the shoes, and the stiff white shirt, diamonds sparkling at the cuffs. I know the type. High achieving, arrogant, not afraid to be unpopular. I look over at Michaela, who's thinking the same thing.

'This one's mine,' I say, and grin at her. 'By the end of the night, I'll have that arrogant stud under the table.'

'Twenty quid says you won't,' Michaela whispers as we take their heavy, quality-tailored coats to the cloakroom.

'You're on,' I snap back, and we go back to take their drinks orders. A faint but unmistakeable aroma of single malt and cigars has permeated the room and they have now taken their seats.

A fair amount of alcohol has obviously already been consumed, but that doesn't prevent a prolonged debate over the frighteningly expensive wine list. We take orders for smoked salmon, quails' eggs and truffle mousse for appetisers. For entrées there are lamb shanks in redcurrant and truffle jus, medallions of pork and, for the big boss, lemon sole caught that day. Apart from him, they are a red-blooded crowd through and through. One of the younger members of the party, in a Paul Smith suit and vivid shirt, obviously worn to eschew conventional dress, pauses and glances up at me.

'I can't see hot waitress on the menu,' he jokes, the first one of the party to chance it with the smart cracks.

'That's a dessert special,' I say smoothly.

'Ah, I see. Can I have a taste to see if I like it?'

'Down boy!' the man next to him says. There's laughter. I smile and move away. It won't do to play their game too soon. Instead I work from one end to the other, removing napkins, placing them in laps.

'Thank you, miss,' the saucy Paul Smith man says, mock innocently. He's in his early thirties, has obviously hit the big time early, and is cocksure of himself in every way, no doubt. There's not a lot of room between the diners, so I have to move quite close to put his napkin in his lap. As I move in, his eyes are directly in line with the top of my much-admired breasts. It'll only take a second for him to grab a ribbon with his teeth and pull, letting them fall free. Obviously he has the imagination to think it as well, as his eyes remain glued to that tempting ribbon. I move to the next man, knowing I left behind a very subtle aroma of Ghost perfume and the idea of what could be ...

Michaela and I give the orders to the kitchen and fetch bottles of carbonated water.

'These blokes are like geysers ready to blow,' Michaela remarks once we are out of earshot. 'I've had my first feel already.'

'No! Who?'

'At the end.' She nods towards an angular-faced man with heavy-lidded eyes. He's whispering to the man next to him, who's grinning. 'No doubt telling him I'm wearing a thong.'

We pour the water and then serve the appetisers, to appreciative murmurs. We cruise around, refilling water and wine glasses. Practice has taught us to know who has what.

'Miss, my napkin has gone missing,' the man next to my friend in Paul Smith calls out in a spoiled, public-school accent. 'I think it's under the table.'

There are sniggers. It is amazing how an attractive face and generous breasts can reduce a man to adolescence. I can see the napkin between his chair and another. It wouldn't take too much effort for him to pick it up, but if he wants me to get on my knees, I have no choice. I can hardly tell him to get it himself. I crouch down and stretch my arm under the table to get the offending scrap of material, allowing him a delicious view of my breasts straining against the ribbon lacing. My skirt, short and flippy, rises dangerously high over my thighs. As I stretch further, I know my stocking tops are exposed, or at least the lacy webbing. I can feel his eyes upon me, sense his desire to run his fingers over my silky flesh, but as I stand up again he smiles coolly.

'Thank you.'

'Don't let it happen again,' I scold him as I place the napkin back in his lap. It doesn't lie quite as smoothly as before, but I choose to ignore it and go back to Michaela.

'We're equals,' I whisper. 'I've just copped my first stiffy.'

We high-five and go back out, this time to clear the plates. There is a heated discussion as to which wine to have with the entrée. At £300 a bottle, the Montrachet isn't cheap, but that doesn't seem to bother them. As Richard, the boss, is having sole he chooses the 1995 Chablis Grand Cru and, again, the price is not an issue. Despite the amount of alcohol he's throwing down his neck, he never offers me more than a wintry smile, and it seems that my bet with Michaela will be lost.

Greg, my Paul Smith man, calls me over yet again. I have been kept busy all evening, with calls for more wine, more water, clean napkins.

'Will you marry me?'

There is laughter, but if he thinks I'm going to blush at his outrageous question, he's destined to be disappointed. I hear this sort of thing all the time.

'I'm sure you're a big pussycat, but the answer's no,' I say sweetly.

'Hey, she says you're a big pussy, Greg. That's the most intelligent thing I've heard all evening!'

I catch Richard's eye and, for some reason, I blush. He's glaring in our direction. I move over to him, away from Greg.

'Is everything to your liking, sir?'

'I would say the asparagus was a little overcooked, but the fish was excellent.' He leans back so I can take his plate. As I do so, I nearly drop it. A hand, cool and light of touch, feathers up my skirt and is stroking the soft, naked skin under my buttocks, just where my stocking top ends and my panties begin.

'Yes, I would say everything was just right,' he says again, as the hand retreats and he gives me a steely smile. I blink, fighting to recover my composure, and bear the plate away, aware that my legs are trembling slightly. This time I don't tell Michaela, who is enjoying a saucy joke with two men on the other side of the room. The bet is still on, and the odds have swung to my favour.

The small room is filled with top-flight small talk. The conversation is of business, of sailing, of good wine and fast cars. Toys for the big boys.

'Let me ask you something,' Piers asks me. I have all their Christian names by now, as they seem eager to give them away. He has dark wavy hair and intense brown eyes, and seems a little more gentlemanly than the others.

'Which do you prefer, Porsche, or a Ford Mondeo?' he asks.

They are grinning, waiting for my answer. I think it over.

'I've already got a Porsche, so why would I need a Mondeo?'

'Bad luck, Piers,' someone jeers.

'Seriously?' He looks disbelieving, yet hopeful.

I laugh, making my hair shimmer in the candlelight. 'I don't need fast cars. I'm fast enough without them,' I say, flashing them all a cheeky look. I reach over him for the wine bottle. He covers the top of his glass.

'Pour it between your tits. I'll drink it from there,' he says boldly.

Strike the gentlemanly bit. I wag my finger at him. 'You are a very bad boy, and deserve a thorough spanking.'

He clasps his hands together in a pleading attitude. 'Oh yes, please!'

I pour his wine. 'Drink. You'll get over it.'

The others are laughing. I pour wine for them as well and disappear into the women's bathroom to cool off. It's getting warm in the dining room, but that could just be the increasingly sexual vibes buzzing around. My face is flushed and, in the sudden chill, my nipples have stiffened like coat hooks. Michaela comes in to tidy her hair. She slips her arm around my waist.

'They're ours for the taking,' she says. 'How are you getting on with Mr Iceman?'

'Deceptively well,' I say, grinning.

'Bullshit! He's probably waiting to get home to his frosty wife to give her a hammering. He'll be thinking of you instead, but he won't play away. It'll cost him too much if she finds out.'

'How would she find out? Anyway, you don't even know if he's married.'

'Honey, you can always tell.' She is now stripping off her blouse and removing her bra. 'Time to unleash the weapons.' From her bag she brings out another bra, this time with quarter-cups, allowing her pert, generous nipples to rest on the top. She gives them a tweak to make them harder still, then slips her blouse back on.

'That is obscene,' I say, admiring her thrusting breasts and perky nipples.

'No worse than you.' She grabs my breasts and plumps them up, so the cleavage is deeper than before, then teases my nipples out with her fingertips. 'Come on, they'll want feeding.'

'Very funny.'

We go to clear the remains of their entrée. There isn't much left. Obviously, the men have healthy appetites. And there are still two courses to go.

First there's dessert, which includes fluffy golden plum soufflés, tiny sticky-toffee puddings and, with predictable ribaldry, spotted dick and custard. Richard has fresh fruit and cheese, I notice. He isn't going to be seen to be indulging, even though he manages to finish a whole bottle of Chablis by himself without anyone noticing. We place the dishes on the table, glancing at each other over the men's heads. We're moving a little closer by this time, making them even more aware of our scent. A hand, placed on the back, can be as sensual as an obvious thrusting of breasts in the face. We want them generous; we want them to impress us with how much they can spend. We are assiduous in placing napkins in laps again, this time brushing ever so slightly against a stomach, or legs, or groin, if we can get away with it. And all the while we keep the wine flowing.

'You know, it would be so easy to sneak under the table and give one of those guys a little pleasure,' Michaela says mischievously.

'You would as well,' I reply. 'Anyway, the real pleasure would be in watching their faces as it was being done.'

'I'd like to watch you doing Mr Iceman,' Michaela murmurs.

'Excuse me! Could you pick up my fork?' It's Greg, the careless one. He is gesturing to the space in front of the table. The fork is laying on the carpet and Michaela bends down to pick it up.

'I've dropped mine as well,' someone says, on the other side of the room. Again, she picks it up. There is applause and cheering and I see immediately what their game is. Every time she bends to pick up the stray cutlery, her skirt rises up and gives the men behind her a perfect view of her creamy backside and lace stocking tops.

Then a spoon lands on the carpet next to my foot. I lean down to get it, aware of my breasts pushing perilously against the stretchy silk blouse, and of my skirt rising, exposing my naked thighs and causing a light breeze to waft across them. That sudden coolness makes my nipples react, pinging to attention as I stand back up. I shake my hair back from my face and waggle the spoon at its owner. It's Piers.

'Do that again, and I'll make you eat with your fingers,' I admonish him.

'Can I eat with yours?' he replies, looking hungrily at my breasts.

What the hell, I think, and stick my finger in the silky crème before proffering it to his lips. He looks slightly stunned, looking around at his colleagues before sucking my finger into his mouth. His eyes close with pleasure.

'Would you like to change to another – perhaps an Armagnac to go with that?' I ask, retrieving my finger. 'Perhaps the *Domaine de Vicbilh*, sir ... it's a 1914.'At £50 a shot, it isn't something to be ordered lightly, but he just nods, an expression of dumb happiness on his face.

We volunteer our choice of after-dinner drinks and work the table, asking each man his order, making suggestions, gently persuading them to go a little higher, a little more expensive. Already drunk and stimulated by our flirting, they agree. When I arrive at Richard's place, he is still perusing the menu. For the second time that evening, his hand slips up my skirt, but this time I don't jump. I move against his fingers, encouraging them to explore further. However, when they do, it's still a shock.

Slim and capable, they find my slick centre and slide in like a hot knife through butter. I am effectively his glove puppet, unable to move.

'I know what you're doing,' he whispers, moving his hand very slightly so I feel weak with desire. 'They don't care, because they don't have to pay for it. But I do, and I like value for money. That's why I'm obscenely wealthy. Do you understand?'

'Yes, sir.' It just comes out, that natural acceptance of authority. I curse my weakness, even though there's not much I can do about it, with his hand where it is. I can feel the crisp cotton cuff chafing my tender flesh, the impersonal sharpness of the diamond cuff link, the soft caress of cashmere wool.

'You want something from me. I want something from you.' He pushes his hand up further, and smiles cruelly at my confused expression. 'You and your hot little friend. I want you to entertain us. For that, I'll pay you the price of each cognac we drink, starting from now.'

'Entertain you? How?' I give him my best wide-eyed look and he uses his hand to draw me hard against him.

'Use your imagination,' he rasps, and removes his hand. As I watch, he sucks his fingers with inestimable finesse and gives me that same cool smile.

'He wants us to do what?' Michaela asks, Hennessy bottle in hand.

'Think about it. How much is that worth?' I motion to the bottle. 'Fifteen hundred? We could make some serious cash.' I glance around the kitchen; it's a lot quieter now. The head chef has already departed, and there is only the residual cleaning up to be done. We won't be disturbed until the club manager breaks things up. And he won't do that until he's sure they aren't going to spend any more money.

'Why the hell not?' Michaela takes a swig from the Hennessy bottle. I grab it from her and do the same.

We walk back into the dining room and clear the remaining dishes, moving the candlesticks to the side tables. There are coffee cups and petits fours, cheese for some of the men, and various liqueurs scattered around the table. Several of the guys are smoking cigars. A dark, smoky, fragrant atmosphere, full of sensual possibilities, permeates the air. Then Michaela and I calmly climb on to the table and stand in the middle, ignoring the men who have stopped talking and are looking at us in amazement. Michaela looks like a sex kitten but she seems shy as I begin to kiss her. Her hesitant reaction is enough to send a frisson of sensual tension throughout the room. When she does relax and respond to my tongue the men sigh as one. I continue to kiss her, holding her face in my hands, planting little kisses all over her eyes, her nose, her lips, before travelling down, tracing her jaw with my tongue, her long, dusky neck. There's an audible sigh as she shimmies her hair back and thrusts out her tiny breasts in their uplifting bra, and ever so slowly I pull the ribbons holding her top together. Instead of pushing the top off her shoulders I kiss her full red lips again, my hands cupping her breasts, thumbs emphasising the nipples. Then down I go, squeezing her buttocks, slowly gathering her swingy short skirt up to her waist, and turning her so the men can appreciate her shapely backside. My fingernails dig into the soft flesh, pushing the honey-coloured globes together, and I can see the men, slack-jawed with lust. I also catch a glance of Richard, watching through steepled fingers, resting back in his chair, his expression inscrutable.

I unzip the skirt and let it fall around her ankles, exposing her completely, her legs long and elegant in seamed black stockings. Her top comes next, draped around her shoulders, then her waist, easing snugly over her hips, and onto the floor. I go behind her and cup her breasts again, showing them to the men, before leaning down to flick at a nipple with my tongue. She isn't expecting that, and gasps with shock as well as pleasure. The men watch avidly as she grows used to the sensation, her nipples yearning to meet my tongue, until they are at full arousal.

'This feels so good,' she gasps as I kiss her velvet-cushioned lips again.

'Easy money,' I murmur.

'Now what?'

'Pour more cognac.'

But Richard has obviously primed them. As we crawl around the table, trying to refill each glass, the answer is the same. Not until we do what they want.

As we move around, doing their bidding, I realise I could never be a lap dancer in real life; I want to be touched too much from getting so turned on by performing. My thighs feel slightly chafed from all the suited laps I have sat on, and

I feel open and needy, my breasts aching and desperate for attention. Michaela is on her front over the table, giggling, with a man apparently devouring her bottom, while another, more high-spirited and obviously kinky bloke is smacking her cheeks until they're red. I am determined to keep my clothes on for now, waiting until I've worked them into a frenzy.

Piers is next. I sit down obediently, leaning back against the table so he can run his hands over my breasts. Between my legs I can feel him, hard and throbbing merrily away, as he rescues some ice from his water and rubs it over my jersey-covered nipples, watching the material grow transparent around them. As he sucks and bites gently I squirm and gasp in delight, and eventually fill his glass again when he allows me to move to the next man. It's Greg, he of the saucy smile and musky aftershave. He has managed to free himself so that when I sit down, it's right on top of hot, naked flesh, rearing up from his expensive black trousers.

'No one will know,' he whispers, as I look around and see he has the tablecloth wrapped discreetly around my bottom. 'I dare you.'

I squeeze him conspiratorially, and he gasps with anticipation.

'You are very naughty,' I say, trying to be severe, but my voice is husky with lust – a dead giveaway. He pushes my breasts together and licks along the deep crevice. He ravishes my breasts, above the neckline of my top, hungrily as if he had not eaten for a month, until someone else tells him he is being greedy. With some regret, I slide away, leaving him bereft, his lips bruised and red with desire. For a while I am lost in a sea of hands and tongues and fingers, all erring on the side of caution, not wanting to be the first to totally unleash their deepest cravings and strip my clothes away.

The Hennessy bottle is nearly empty by the time I finish moving around the table, so I fill another glass and pour some of the golden alcohol between Michaela's breasts as she lays across the table, bending down to lick it back up. Then I flow it over her nipples, following the cool liquid with a hot tongue, vying for it with a man who is desperately trying to do the same.

'Stop!' Richard's firm voice resounds through the room. He is standing up, a little unsteadily, it has to be said, but standing, and lucid, and determined. He motions to the space on the tablecloth in front of him.

'Lie down,' he says to me. To Michaela he says, 'Carry on.'

With the low voice of Nina Simone in the background, and the lights even lower, I lie on the table, aware of twelve pairs of eyes roaming all over my body. Richard sits back in his chair, savouring his single vintage Hennessy and his Monte Cristo, occasionally blowing a smoke ring our way. Michaela is hesitant at first, her kisses perfunctory, but as her tongue becomes eager, her hands bolder, I find myself squirming under her touch, my hands reaching for the cloth beneath me, my back arching as my breasts ache for her kiss. Swollen with need for a good tongue-lashing, they seem to take over my whole being. I hold my breath, willing them to rise up even more, to have attention lavished upon them, but just as Michaela moves towards them, Richard tells her to stop again.

'With your teeth,' he says, motioning to the ribbons. So she slowly, agonisingly, teases the ribbons loose, letting my poor, sensitive breasts push their way to freedom. Finally my damp top is peeled away, and my nipples spring joyfully towards the cooler air, only to be held cruelly back by my tiny bra. My breasts swell upwards and, as Michaela finally removes my bra and lets them loose at last, I am aware of an admiring murmur among the men. This is what they want – to see me bare-breasted and rolling around in a state of arousal on a dining table. As Michaela curls her tongue around a nipple with frustrating slow licks, my lower body is out of control, undulating of its own free will. Little gasps of frustration escape my lips; so much for being in control! As I meet

Richard's smile I almost admit defeat, but Michaela moves down and begins to press hot little kisses over my stomach, gradually easing the small skirt over my curvaceous thighs. There are shouts of appreciation at my transparent black panties, with their sprigs of pink roses. Then she moves down, trailing the bare skin above my stocking tops with her tongue. My legs part wantonly as she moves towards my cleft, and there's a groan as she pushes her face right into it. The groan comes from me. I wasn't expecting that, the bad girl.

Someone has sent downstairs for champagne, and a bottle of Veuve Clicquot La Grande Dame is produced for Richard. He promptly pours it over my nipples, making them tingle deliciously. The cool fluid falls in rivulets down my body, pools in my navel, spreads cold fingers around my ribs and drips on to the cloth below. He bends his head to drink from my personal well of champagne.

'You're going to pay dearly for all of this,' I warn him.

'So, my dear, are you.' He drains his glass and lets me drink the remains of his champagne, straight from his mouth to mine. Apart from the small swig of Hennessy, it's the first drink I have had all evening and it feels like sweet nectar on my tongue. His taste, of cigars and cognac and expensive champagne, is intoxicating, and right then I will do anything for him, without reason, as I am so turned on. Realising this, I see the implied warning in his words. In my left hand I am aware of a deep pulsing, like the engine of a super-charged sports car. He has manoeuvred my hand into his lap. I feel for his zip and work my way in through the soft cashmere wool trousers, gasping into his mouth as I find him, naked and aggressively hard. Michaela eases my panties away and spreads my legs. I yelp as I feel her tongue, flickering as delicately as a snake would taste for prey. My right hand, not my own any more, curves around another upstanding male member. I vaguely register the men fully dressed, but somehow obscene, stroking themselves, watching us hungrily, one climbing on the table behind Michaela as she concentrates on me. Her movements become more forceful, controlled by the man behind her, giving her everything he has. Liquid trickles into my mouth, sweet, cool and fizzy. Champagne. Bring it on, I think, as pleasure swells and peaks, swells and peaks, over and over, in response to the rhythmic flicking of Michaela's tongue. As I crash and burn into orgasm my hand tightens around Richard. Too carried away by the scenario in front of him to resist, he loses control, the exquisite agony ripping across his face. I smile up at him triumphantly, feeling viscous liquid trickle over my breasts. Michaela is borne away by the four who have not got a look in before. Their mingled groans are soft and urgent in the darkest part of the room. Richard slumps in his chair, drained and sated, too exhausted to cover himself properly.

'I'll bring you the bill, sir,' I say smoothly, skipping to my feet.

He signs the tab with a flourish, without wincing, and produces a fat wad of notes from inside his jacket.

'Give these to Michaela. She did well tonight,' he says. He grins vividly for the first time. 'You'll get yours when you get home, you dirty girl.'

3

Steam heat

It was shaping up to be one of those memorable summers – where we got a good few consecutive days of sizzling sun, without the insane humidity and eventual thunderclouds. I had nothing to do but laze by the pool at my friend Suzanne's house, waiting for the day when I was to start working again. That was two weeks away, so I intended to make the most of the weather, lounging with a book and looking up into the blue sky that made me feel so alive and optimistic. My tan was looking good, a warm honey gold that complemented my light blonde hair. Because the pool was at the back of the house, with trees around the garden perimeter, we could strip off completely, although that day we were in bikinis because Suzanne was waiting for a mobile valet to arrive and didn't want to give him any more of a shock than was necessary.

He was to give Suzanne's boyfriend's Mercedes a much needed clean and polish. Suzanne's bloke was expected back home in two days after a three-week business trip, and in that time she had managed to trash the inside and spill Coke on the front passenger seat.

She had parked the car in the shade around the back of the

garage, ostensibly so that the valet wouldn't have to polish it in the full blazing sun. That was very considerate, I said, but it meant we'd have to keep our tops on for the afternoon when I'd planned to get the best of the sun on my breasts. I love the feel of the sun on my naked flesh, showering its rays on the soft sensitive skin of my nipples. It always makes them hard, and lying in the sun always makes me really turned on. Especially afterwards, when I've showered and treated my body with some rich, sensual lotion and slipped on some of my favourite underwear. With glittering strappy sandals and a slinky thin dress, I always know I look good on those summer evenings. I was snapped out of my indulgent reverie by Suzanne saying, 'It's a small price to pay.'

I saw the mischievous smile on her face. From our sun loungers, we had a perfect view of the car.

'Oh, I get it. He's pretty fit, then,' I said.

'You got it.' Suzanne grinned. We clinked our Pimm's glasses together. Sun, shimmering blue water, and an uninterrupted view of a man working up a sweat. Couldn't be better.

He came an hour later, in a little white van with STEVE McCLEAN – MOBILE VALET written on the side. As Suzanne took him into the kitchen for a drink I slipped on my Jimmy Choos, tied a filmy sarong around my waist, and sauntered into the dark, cool house to join them. Suzanne was fixing him a long glass of water filled with tinkling ice cubes. She picked it up, holding the glass level with her breasts, so he could not help noticing them.

'You want lemon?' she asked.

'No thanks.' He licked his lips, watching the condensation run down the glass, onto her hand. I hid a smile. Suzanne made flirting an art form.

She handed him the glass, and it was then he noticed me. His eyes widened as if he couldn't believe his luck, and then he gave a lopsided grin that was almost a smirk, but not quite.

'There'll be two of us making sure you're working hard today,' Suzanne said. 'Abs, this is Tony.'

'Er, not Steve, then?' I looked out the window at the name on his van.

'That's the company name. As in Steve McQueen. *The Magnificent* ...' he was staring at my breasts '. . . *Seven*.'

'Right,' I said, amused at the way he was trying to tear his gaze away from my chest. I was used to it, and that day it was on display more than usual, thanks to my tiny white frilled bikini top, which just about covered the nipples and not much more. I was doing some ogling as well. Tony wore a tight white T-shirt, slightly smeared with car dirt, which enhanced his tanned, muscled arms, and even tighter black jeans. There was only one reason a man would wear jeans like that in temperatures topping eighty degrees, and it was obvious that he fancied Suzanne like mad. It was equally obvious that neither of them had done anything about it yet. There was more than a *frisson* of sexual tension in the air, like the atmosphere before an impending storm.

'So which wheels are we doing today?' Tony asked, trying to recover from the shock of seeing two stunning girlies in minimal clothing. He had a chirpy London accent, and there was a slight arrogance about his manner, as if he resented the respect he had to give his wealthy female customers. I could tell from his attitude that he reckoned himself as the Mac Daddy of motors. He had short, dark hair, fashioned into a spiky quiff, which made him look tough and a little threatening, even though, in my heels, I was a couple of inches taller than him. As he and Suzanne walked past me I could smell a musky aftershave and the unmistakeable aroma of warm male. Suzanne winked at me and grinned. I knew that grin. It meant, let's have some fun with this sucker.

We went back to our chairs and watched him set up his equipment: the high-powered water jet, the industrial-sized vacuum cleaner, and a box full of polishes, waxes, car shampoos and upholstery cleaners. We sipped our Pimm's and soaked up the sun, listening to the radio and talking about Suzanne's recent trip to the Caribbean.

Tony was vacuuming the car, clearing out the remains of fast-food wrappers and Coke cans.

'You're such a slut,' I murmured to Suzanne, as I watched the amount of rubbish coming out.

'It's in my nature,' she replied, sucking at her straw. She was watching Tony from behind her Gucci shades. His tight backside moved back and forth as he worked the vacuum cleaner. I wondered whether he was aware of us eyeing him up.

For almost an hour he went at it, his T-shirt gradually becoming damp between the shoulder blades. Finally, he slammed the car door.

'You want another Pimm's?' Suzanne asked.

I had had two already, and that and the warmth of the sun was making me feel a little woozy. As she went to make some more I kicked off my shoes and unknotted my sarong, ready to slip into the water.

As the filmy material fell to my feet I was aware of Tony watching me, so I shook my hair back from my face and stretched to show my curvy figure to its full advantage. As I turned, he was treated to a view of my almost naked bottom in the white bikini bottoms, before I stepped into the water and pushed away from the side. The water seemed cooler than the last time I had been in, and I had to swim a couple of lengths to get comfortable before I could paddle around and play with the Lilo that was bobbing about in the middle. I couldn't get up on it gracefully, although I did think about straddling the plastic, pushing my bum up a little, just out of the water, to give Tony an eyeful of gorgeous girl flesh. In the end, I felt a little shy, and instead walked back up the stairs, swaying my hips a little, my white bikini rendered almost transparent by the water.

'Warm in there?' he called. He had been watching me the

whole time, but dared not come any closer. I was glad I hadn't tried to get up on the Lilo.

'Nice and cool,' I called back, subtly arching my back so he would better notice my perky nipples. Suzanne came tottering back on her platform espadrilles with a full jug of Pimm's and two fresh glasses. Slices of cucumber, strawberry and mint leaves floated around on top.

'Blimey, Suze, we'll be pissed if we drink all that,' I said, but reached for my glass anyway. Suzanne picked up my bottle of tanning oil and poured some into her hand.

'Lie back. I'll do you.'

She reached for the front-fastening clasp on my bikini. I stopped her.

'What do you think you're doing?'

'Oh, relax! Give him something to look at.' She cocked her head at Tony, who had reluctantly turned back to give the alloy wheels a good scrub. I shrugged, and removed the bikini top. We were accustomed to being naughty together. Why should today be any different?

We settled back to watch Tony spraying the car with water. As the spray hit the hot metal, small rainbows shot out in every direction. He took a sponge and began lathering the car with creamy bubbles, rubbing it with such sensuous care I began to feel a little like a rubdown myself. I wanted to lather my breasts with the soap, then have him do it for me. But that might be too much for him, too soon, and I giggled at the thought of him not being able to contain himself. As he reached for the middle of the roof, the motion of his hips was vaguely sexual. I could imagine those tight buns pumping like pistons, and the sheer energy that was driving them, and thought that his girlfriend, if he had one, was a very lucky woman indeed.

His T-shirt became wetter, accentuating the dark patch of hairs on his chest and the small nipples poking through the wet cotton. Suzanne and I looked at each other over the tops of our sunglasses.

'Very nice,' she purred. 'Too good to waste, I would say.'

'What would Jason say?' I whispered. As far as I knew, she had never played around before. But then again, knowing her, she might have.

'He's hardly going to find out,' Suzanne drawled, sucking suggestively on her straw. 'If he did suspect anything, I would say it was you.'

'Thanks.' I thought for a moment. 'Of course, it doesn't have to be a total lie, does it?'

We had talked about it before, but choosing the right candidate had proved difficult. They were either too arrogant, or too grubby (a girl did have limits, after all) or too controlling to allow us to do what we wanted.

'I think we've found him,' I said. Behind my shades, I watched Tony as Suzanne began applying the tanning oil to my body. She started on my stomach. As a professional masseuse, she knew what she was doing. I sighed contentedly and let her get on with it. She moved down to my thighs, lifting one up and bending my knee so she could get to the underside.

'I could turn over,' I suggested, as my thighs fell apart.

'Yeah, well, I want those tight jeans to get even tighter,' she said, her fingers working up, almost to the top of my thigh, then back down, towards my knees. 'Is he looking?'

'He's trying not to,' I said. He did seem to be giving the other alloy wheel a lot of attention.

Down to my feet she worked her magic, her hands warm and slippery with oil, until the whole of my lower body glistened.

'Now the bit I've been looking forward to,' she said, rubbing her hands together. She made a double grabbing motion and we both giggled, causing him to look up. Now we really had his attention. Instead of pouring the oil into her hand she raised it up and let a thin trickle pour down on to my breasts. It sparkled in the sun, like molten gold, coiling first around one nipple, before trailing towards the other. Despite myself, I gasped and arched my back.

'Horny girl,' she said, her fingers smoothing over my skin. Tony had a perfect view as I lay, my head between her breasts, as she reached down for mine. Gathering them up, she let her fingers ease over my caramel skin. My body rippled as she massaged the oil in, concentrating around my nipples, teasing them out until they were huge and pink, like juicy raspberries.

'Oh, he's off,' she whispered. I opened my eyes to see Tony walking back towards the house.

'Where's he going?' I asked.

Suzanne shrugged. 'To have a whiz, probably. Or a wank. Who knows? Anyway, it's my turn.'

With some difficulty, as I was so relaxed, and probably a little tipsy, I eased myself to a position where I could still lie down but rub oil into Suzanne's back at the same time. She rolled over to her front and pulled her bikini bottoms down under her buttocks. They were full and their texture was so enticing it was difficult not to get carried away. I let the oil trickle between the crevice, making them wobble invitingly, before smoothing the unguent over them.

'I thought you said it's a shame to waste it?' I pointed out. Her skin began to glisten as I worked in the oil, down her legs, up her back, untying her bikini top to get at her smooth, silky back.

'Yeah, but if he's a real man ...'

'All the same, maybe I should go check,' I said. 'I've got all my jewellery in there.'

A movement from the kitchen had caught my eye moments before. I knew that Tony was in there, watching us. The thought that he was feasting his eyes on us in secret made me hotter than ever. Why did he need to go into the kitchen? Was he too turned on to continue working?

'Turn over,' I said to Suzanne. As she obligingly did so, exposing her breasts to the sun, I poured more oil into my hands, warmed it up, and covered her breasts with it. They felt deliciously warm and soapy under my touch, the nipples springy and responsive. She bit her lip and sighed as I bent down and pressed my lips against one, firming it even more. The taste of coconut was faint but unmistakeable on my tongue.

'Have some fun. I'll be back in a minute,' I whispered, guiding Suzanne's hand down, towards the vee between her legs. The gold material was puckered slightly, emphasising her soft, hairless cleft. Sleepily she did as she was told, her finger pushing underneath the stretchy material to form an almost phallic-looking ridge.

As she became involved in pleasuring herself I slipped away and crept, shoeless this time, into the house. Sure enough, at the kitchen window, Tony was there, his lips parted, his chest heaving slightly. Further down, his jeans were open, and his hand was moving slowly, deliberately. There was no hurry, no frantic desperation, just sheer enjoyment at the sight before him.

I backed away out of the kitchen, silently, and walked back to the poolside as if nothing had happened. I poured more Pimm's, picked the glass up and rubbed it over my breasts, turning slightly towards the kitchen so he could see their profile, upturned and perky, before sucking more of the innocuously fruity cocktail. I was feeling rather daring, and Suzanne looked very tempting, laid out on the lounger like a banquet waiting to be plundered. I nudged over the other lounger and lay down next to her, letting my fingers drift over her stomach.

'He's in there, giving himself a long, slow hand-shandy,' I said softly.

Suzanne opened one eye. 'Then I think it's time, don't you?'

I went back into the house first, calling out, 'Tony, do you want another drink?'

As I walked back into the kitchen he was frantically trying to zip up his jeans.

'Oh!' I said, feigning surprise. My eyes widened as I looked downwards. His underpants were up, but his tight jeans had been his downfall. He was too aroused for the zip to go back up, and the accusing evidence pushed aggressively through the gap beneath the button on his waistband.

For a moment, we stared at each other. His erection had begun to wilt with the shock, but when I put my hands on my hips, and thrust out my breasts towards him, it stalled and began to grow again. Suzanne appeared behind me.

'Well!' she said, peeling off her glasses to feast her eyes on him. 'What do we have here?'

'Look, girls,' he blustered. 'What do you expect? All that touching and rubbing. Any man would ...'

'Are you any man?' Suzanne raised a dark eyebrow. 'I was hoping you weren't!'

Tony looked confused. His eyes shifted from Suzanne to me, and back again. I could tell he was hoping, but not believing what was about to happen to him.

'The T-shirt should come off first,' she said.

'Oh, definitely,' I agreed, nodding.

We folded our arms, and waited. Tony laughed nervously. We nodded in unison. Eventually he peeled it off, like the skin off a ripe fruit. His stomach was hard and flat, his chest broad and well defined under a silky patch of hair. We ushered him outside and gave him his orders.

'Now rinse the car again and start lathering it down,' Suzanne said.

'He should take his jeans off as well,' I pointed out. 'He can't do them up, anyway. And it seems a shame to waste those nice white Calvins.'

He looked at us as if we were mad, but there was no wriggling out of it. He turned around, stripped off his jeans, and put his trainers back on, to protect his feet from the gravel.

'Get the hose,' Suzanne said to me. 'He needs a clean as well.'

'I could get in the pool,' he offered, somewhat hopefully.

'I mean a real clean.' She turned the hose on to a softer spray and began to shower him with it. He yelled in protest.

But when I approached him with the sponge filled with soapy water he gave in. I pushed him over the bonnet of the Mercedes and began to lather him all over. Every time our bodies slid together, a jolt of electricity shot through us both. I wriggled against him, playing my breasts against his soapy chest, naughtily letting my nipples brush against his own. For a brief moment, he grabbed my buttocks and pressed hard against me, grazing my lower belly with his thrusting heat, but it was a fleeting, frustrating caress that left us both highly aroused, before Suzanne played the hose over him again. Standing away, I enjoyed the sight of his erection, clear and pinkly visible through the now sodden, translucent Calvin Klein trunks. It was an incredibly erotic sight. Then Suzanne threw the chamois leather at him.

'Now get to work,' she growled.

It took him a long time to get every drop of water off the car. We watched his body as he stretched and rubbed and exerted himself, feeling as if we were having the same sort of work-out ourselves. All I could think about was that promising packet in his briefs.

'Keep him distracted,' Suzanne said, as he bent to rub down the boot and back bumper. I stood close, so he could see my long, shapely legs and sparkly stilettos, my toenails pink and freshly pedicured. While I was flashing him my legs, Suzanne got inside the car. Tony started to work on the roof. As the car was wide he had a job to reach, and was leaning at full stretch. I saw the window slide open in front of him and I knew then what Suzanne planned to do. I picked up another chamois leather, soft and supple.

'You can do better than that,' I said, and whupped his backside with the leather. As it smacked satisfyingly against his backside he grunted, thrusting against the open car window. His irritation turned to shock as Suzanne hooked a finger into his soaking pants and deftly sucked him into her mouth. He sagged against the car, moaning, 'Oh, fuck.' I slapped his arse with the leather again.

'Come on, Tony, do your job!'

He shot me an evil look and crawled back upright, stretching over the car with the leather. Again I hit him, and again Suzanne was waiting. This time he was ready with an eager thrust of his hips. As he continued to polish that paintwork, Suzanne continued to fellate him. I peeled down his Calvins to reveal a beautifully round, firm backside, which I eagerly grabbed and fondled, this time rubbing my hot body against his back. It was so stimulating being this wicked with a man so helpless and at our mercy that I could feel myself getting very steamed up down below. He gave up leathering the car to just enjoy the twin sensations, moaning against the hot car roof, his shallow breath leaving little puffs of moisture on the metal.

'I'm losing it,' he muttered.

'No, you're not,' I said, turning him around so he didn't suddenly go too far in Suzanne's mouth. His eyes were glassy, still slightly disbelieving, as if he were in a dream he didn't want to wake up from. Suzanne got out of the car and appeared beside us.

'He still hasn't finished,' she said, but I believe in giving a guy a break.

'Come with us,' I said, and just in case he decided that wasn't what he wanted to do (which was highly unlikely) I curled my hand around the thick rod of flesh sticking out in front of him and tugged, leading him towards the pool. He completely removed his Calvins and followed dutifully.

'Now you can have a dip,' I said.

I could tell that going in the pool wasn't the kind of dip he had in mind, but he kicked off his trainers anyway.

'You coming in?' he asked. He didn't really trust us, but

there wasn't anything else we could do while he was in the pool.

'In a minute,' I said. 'You go ahead and swim. I want to see two lengths. Backstroke.' I grinned at Suzanne. She nodded. We sipped our Pimm's and watched approvingly as he did as he was told. His technique wasn't brilliant but it didn't matter. We were watching his muscled body, and that enormous appendage rearing out of the water like a rude pink rudder. When he had finished, Suzanne stood by the side of the pool.

'You can come out now,' she said.

But he shook his head. His dark hair stuck to his scalp and spiked across his forehead. He clambered up on the Lilo and lay on it on his back, his legs trailing the water.

'No way. You want me, you come here.' He glanced down his body, and grinned at us, knowing exactly what we wanted. We looked at each other. This wasn't part of the plan. Somehow, we had to regain control.

I was feeling decidedly tipsy, and when I was tipsy, I always pushed my boundaries just a little further than I would otherwise. This time, I sat on the side of the pool, with my legs in the water. I reclined back on the hot stone, and eased my bikini bottoms aside, exposing the pouting lips of my cleft.

'You want me, you come here,' I said, in a sultry voice. His erection bobbed and grew. Suzanne came over and pressed her lips against mine. Our tongues curled in an open, pornographic kiss as her fingers walked over my nipples. The next thing I knew, firm hands were on my legs, widening them. He hadn't put up much of a fight, then. There was a trickle of cool as Tony let some Pimm's fall from his lips on to my bud before lapping it up with far more finesse that I had expected from someone like him. I opened my mouth to gasp and felt a straw against my lips. I sucked greedily, knowing it would be my downfall the next day but not caring. I drained the glass, feeling the alcohol fizz around my bloodstream, mingling with the heat from the afternoon sun, and the hot stone burning my back and buttocks. I just opened my legs and let it all happen; my eyes closed, even as I felt Suzanne's body just above mine, naked and salty. I licked my lips and felt hers, smooth and velvety. I reached up with my tongue and tasted musk. It was lovely, intoxicating and flavoured with a hint of coconut. I delved further, knowing I was drunk and just giving in to my every impulse. There was a deep groan, which could have been Suzanne or Tony as my body began to churn with unadulterated pleasure. My tongue mirrored the actions of his, flicking over me. Suzanne's thighs kept me firm against her. I grabbed Tony's hair as he did the same. The heat was all-enveloping, almost unbearable, yet my lower body was in free fall, stretched as wide as it could go. My need verged on a scream. Suzanne moaned louder. She clutched at me, held me, then threw her head back in a glorious surrender to her orgasm. I clawed at Tony, feeling myself hit the heights too, as the molten sensation of exquisite release shot through my sex. And we girls rode every wave, every glorious peak until we were through.

Gasping, Tony fell away. Suzanne sprawled on the white stone, moaning, her hand working those last little tremors.

When I opened my eyes, Tony was out of the pool standing over me, dripping, and still erect. Sparkling drops of water sprinkled my overheated body. Suzanne was lying nearby, open, waiting. It was his choice. He was touching himself, making himself even harder, staring into my eyes.

'It's so hot,' she said. 'It's not often one gets the chance to roll around naked outside. Let's make the most of it.'

With that invitation, Suzanne pulled Tony down on to the concrete and I found myself watching at close range as he wasted no time in getting himself tucked tightly between her legs. He let out a roar of joy as he slid into her, and I was feeling bereft at this point, wanting to experience the sensation of a thick penis in my own needy body. It felt like an age since I had seen Tony's cock through the transparent briefs, and I bit on my lip as I slipped a hand down on myself and clenched it in anticipation.

In the middle of this sweet torture, the phone began to ring. I answered it, hoping my voice would not sound too slurred.

'Hey, how are you?'

It was Jason and, from the clarity of the line, he wasn't in the South Pacific.

'Hey, I'm fine, Jason. Having a good business trip?' I asked. I stood up and walked away from the rutting couple, so that the unmistakeable sounds of heavy-duty copulating would not travel down the line. I saw Suzanne's head poke out from underneath her bit of extra curricular with an expression of panic – blind and total – clouding her face.

Wickedly, I countered her desperate anticipation to know where he was by turning my back on them and walking further away, down the side of the pool. She would kill me afterwards, but I was going to have my own back for not being given a slice of the Tony pie.

On that note, why was he taking so long? Most guys that had been that aroused for that long wouldn't last five minutes.

'Actually, I'm back,' continued Jason. 'Just got into Heathrow. Is Suzanne there?'

I looked over to her and pointed at the phone, then gestured at here. Her response was to wave frantically 'no' with a pleading expression. I wasn't that cruel.

'No, she's ... gone out,' I said.

'Is everything all right? You sound a bit strange.'

'Oh, I'm fine,' I chirped gaily. The hesitant tone to my voice must have come from my mind being on whether I was going to be allowed a turn with Tony before it was all over. 'She'll be home in a while, probably by the time you get back,' I said. A blindingly brilliant thought hit me. 'I'm just here to look after the car valet.'

Jason laughed. 'Don't tell me she's trashed it again?'

'Well ... kinda.'

'I'll see you in a couple of hours,' Jason said. 'Oh, and it's OK, I know your little secret.'

My stomach did a somersault. 'What do you mean?' I squeaked.

'I can tell you've been at the Pimm's.' Laughing, he hung up.

Breathless with relief, even though I wasn't guilty of anything, I leaped back over to Suzanne and Tony.

'That was Jason,' I said. 'He's coming home in a couple of hours.'

Suzanne suddenly looked panicky. 'What did you tell him?'

'That you were fucking on the floor, but you'd call him when you were done.' I said it in a way that implied I assumed they had an open relationship.

At first she looked stricken, already kissing goodbye to the fancy car, the swanky house, the pool, and going back to her flat in Fulham. I enjoyed her pain for a moment before grinning. Inside I felt a little mean, but the greedy cow deserved it.

'Relax, I told him you were out. So if I were you, I'd make yourself scarce for at least an hour, and have some champagne ready for his return, together with a damned good reason for leaving me here.'

'Thanks, honey. I owe you.'

'Well, how about you start by letting me finish off what you started?'

I placed my soft hand in the small of Tony's back, tracing a finger down to the top of his bottom cleft. Emboldened by the drink and the heat, I slid it even further down, until I reached the fuzz of his balls – which clenched in response. I reckoned he was nearing the brink.

'Sorry, mate,' said Suzanne to Tony. 'But I'm sure my friend can help you with the final stages.'

'Twos up? My favourite,' he said, sounding delighted as he wriggled out of Suzanne, his cock red and shining.

When I finally felt the touch of his warm hands on my shoulders I almost melted. I was long overdue the embrace of full-on sex and the feel of a fit bloke on top of me. There was something delicious about the anonymity of it. We'd had a lot of fun with Tony this afternoon and he he's been very compliant and patient with our tipsy demands. Now we were both going to get our reward for patience.

Suzanne hurried back inside the house, probably relieved that she wouldn't have to angst about being really unfaithful by going all the way. I know what she's like.

Meanwhile, I relaxed into the knowledge that I was going to be enjoying myself thoroughly for the next 15 minutes – if Tony lasted that long!

Tony looked me in the eyes then let his gaze roam all over my body with the dirtiest expression on his face. There was little point talking; we both knew what we wanted. Still, I couldn't help saying 'I think you've done really well holding out all this time.'

'Only 'cos I wanted to have a go at you, too.'

'Get out, you cheeky sod,' I teased. 'You were about to blow back there when I tickled your balls.'

'I'm about to blow now, love.'

And as he grabbed himself I felt a rush of lust. The sight of his stiffness and the long-awaited pleasure was driving me nuts. I faltered as he took my hand, and pressed it hard against his cock. His breath caught as I squeezed the hardness I found there. He moved in, and whispered, 'I've always wanted to do it with a gorgeous blonde in a rich man's swimming pool.'

I smiled, and didn't mention mine and Suzanne's fantasy about taking an ordinary bloke and turning him into a sex god for the afternoon, which, in effect, we had accomplished. I led the way into the pool, easing myself off the side and luxuriating in the cool water. It was that time in the afternoon when long shadows were cast over lawns and the sun turns a burnished copper. Much later and the temperature would drop. It was the perfect time for a late afternoon livener to refresh me for the evening.

As soon as he was in the water our bodies drew to each other like magnets. I've always loved messing around with men in swimming pools and in the sea. It makes me feel especially sexy as the water eddies around my breasts and buoys them up to maximum lift. With Tony's confident hands around my waist, I gave myself over to him completely, curling my legs around his waist and waiting for the moment when I would feel him inside me. And it arrived, with full force. He was so, so ready to let go. We looked deeply into each other's eyes as he thrust his desire ever closer to the limit. He held me weightless in the water as fully indulged ourselves to maximum joy.

'I can't hold back any longer,' he croaked, his breath ragged. 'Please, please, can I come inside you?'

Nice of him to ask, I thought. I held my head on one side as if I were debating what shoes to wear. I held him in suspense until the slightest movement would set him off. 'Oh, all right, then,' I teased.

But even if I had forbidden him his moment of ultimate pleasure, it would have been too late. He tensed and flexed his hips and threw his head back, gasping and crying out his triumph.

'Oh, oh, oh,' he shouted into the vast expanse of air above us, his orgasm as vocal as I'd ever heard any man's. I liked it; it showed his enthusiasm.

Despite having climaxed earlier, I was ready again; he'd really got me going, this 'regular guy'. I sneaked a hand down and rubbed myself madly, giddy with the hedonistic escapades of the day. I was pleased to see that Tony stuck around in the water with me while I had my moment of ultimate please, whispering encouraging dirty things in my ear that drove me wild and to the edge much quicker. I love to hear a man talking dirty, while everything surrounding me is clean and luxurious.

I came hard, clutching with one hand at the skin of his shoulders and the other on the side of the pool. He seemed to enjoy that at close range, looking into my face, as he did having his own pleasure.

'That's why I think simultaneous orgasms are a waste,' was the first thing he said once we were finished. 'I can never see a woman enjoying her own if I'm wrapped up with losing it myself.'

He certainly gave me something to think about.

Then, a shadow passed across us. It was Suzanne in a fresh-as-a-daisy linen dress brandishing a fist full of notes for Tony.

'Thanks, babe,' she said.

I'm not sure if she meant me or him. Her little Polo's engine was running and she was ready to make a dash for it.

'If Jason arrives back before I do, tell him I had to see my sister. Relationship crisis. I'll bring back some champagne. And probably some new shoes.'

And with that she backed out of the hard standing and roared off down the driveway, waving one slim brown arm in a cheerful wave.

I pulled myself out of the water and reached for a towel that was lying on the sun lounger. In a matter of minutes our sex god cum regular guy was dressed and gone and all I had to do was shower and dress for the evening, ready to greet Jason when he arrived. It was very naughty, but I wondered how he might look with transparent pants!

4

For Our Eyes Only

He greets me with a megawatt smile as bright as his short-cropped golden hair as I walk through the door. Bounding up the stairs ahead of me, in jeans and his trademark white Ralph Lauren shirt, he exudes enthusiastic energy. The main studio is bright and white, filled with complicated equipment and props. The make-up artist gives me a friendly greeting, and I relax a little.

As my make-up is being applied, Danny and I talk about the shoot, which is for a glossy male magazine. They have asked for tastefully erotic shots with an edge, just what their readership likes, but because he is so good at his job they have given him free rein to do what he sees fit.

As we are talking, another girl enters the room. There is no mistaking it's the second model. She's taller than me, as slender as I am curvy, and absolutely gorgeous in figure-hugging Miss Sixty jeans, a wide studded belt and a flimsy handkerchief-point Boho-style chiffon top.

'This is Helena,' Danny says, introducing us.

'Honey, you look divine,' she says, and genuinely seems to mean it. It is the first shock of the morning. The second is her smile, as feminine and sensual as the golden hair cascading down her back. Her accent is rich and husky, making me wish I had paid more attention to my language classes at school, and her laugh is throaty and sexy. I know Danny will want to convey some of that smouldering sensuality into his shots. Somehow, I have a hunch they'll be really special.

Wrapped in robes, with our faces exquisitely made up with glossy red lipstick and smoky eye shadow, we go into the studio itself.

The shoot is an expensive one; Danny's always are. His studio occupies an old Victorian terrace and each of the rooms has been transformed into a different set. The large bathroom could feature in a costume drama set in a stately home. The walls and floor are swathed in satin, the same wine-red shade as our lipstick, and in the middle of the room, with the satin gathered all around it, is a white china bath with claw-and-ball feet and brass taps at one end. I peer into it.

'I hope that's warm water,' I say, frowning.

'Of course it is. So get naked and get in.'

All thoughts of sitting for hours in freezing cold water dissipate as I see Helena in all her naked glory. She has tiny, high breasts with large, pink nipples. Her eyes widen when she catches sight of my breasts, much fuller but just as firm.

'Darling! Beautiful!' she exclaims, feeling one in her hand as if testing for ripeness. 'And real!'

'One hundred per cent genuine,' I say, feeling pleased she noticed. 'Yours are lovely too,' I say, but restrain myself from touching, though an opportunity will present itself shortly – I hope.

'And such bones! You are like ... a cat. Feline, yet soft. Such a doll.' She traces her finger around my face. It is like being stroked with a lightly charged electric wire.

'Thanks,' I say again, colouring slightly under her direct blue gaze. I hadn't expected her to be so frank, and so soon at that. 'I won't tell you how gorgeous you are, because it's kind of stating the obvious.'

She laughs out loud. 'When you have a gift, you must use it well.'

I decide I like Helena a lot.

As Danny promised, the bath water is warm but not hot, as he doesn't want any unsightly red marks to show up on the photographs. Bubbles rise over the rim of the bath as we settle in. Immediately we begin flipping the creamy bubbles back and forth, giggling at the strangeness of the situation. Helena is obviously enjoying herself as much as I am. Bubbles land in our hair, on our faces, and on the satin the bath is standing on.

Danny comes over and rearranges the bubbles over our breasts, so just the nipples are peeking through. I keep an eye on his crotch. There is a generous bulge and he's not even hard yet.

Helena flirtatiously flips bubbles at him. He smiles and murmurs at her to behave, but he doesn't specify exactly how. I lie back in the water and mentally strip him bare, imagining all sorts of naughty things happening, like him doing the remainder of the shoot in his underpants. Yes, that would be good. He would be stuck behind the camera while Helena and I wash each other and play with each other's breasts in front of the lens, out of reach.

'OK, are you happy about touching each other?' he asks eventually.

'You mean, like this?' Helena says. She gathers my breasts up and proffers them to him. 'Or like this?' She moves around until she is behind me. Danny is clicking away as she draws me back against her so I can feel nipples tickling my shoulders. And as she wriggles against me her warm, soapy breasts slide up and down my back.

'How does that feel?' Danny asks, as his camera clicks furiously like a mating insect.

I smile into his eyes. 'Wonderful. They feel so firm. And silky.' I move sensuously against Helena, enjoying the weight and pressure of her bust on my slippery skin, and gasp as a sly finger works its way between my legs. As my nipples reawaken, crinkling and growing before Danny's eyes, the reaction in his jeans is immediate and very noticeable. My gaze flickers towards it, then back up to his face. Message is received and understood. What's more, he is using it to coax us. Helena is stroking me very gently, flooding me with a host of dizzying sensations. I would be very happy to stay there and let her take me wherever at will, but Danny picks up two large black towels and tells us to get out of the water.

'You'll get all pruney,' he says, clearing his throat with a cough. 'Dry each other off. Abs, you go first.'

Fighting my frustration, I do as I'm bid, bending down before Helena to dab the moisture and bubbles away from her pale skin. She arches her back, letting her hair fall down almost to her buttocks, and there is such a look of rapture on her face that I wonder what kind of primal Germanic forces would be unleashed when she climaxed.

When she dries me, she runs the soft towel lovingly over my stomach and thighs, turning me around so my back is to the camera. Her tongue is warm and unexpected in the crevice of my buttocks. They quiver as she nips me gently, not enough to raise a mark, but enough for me to feel her small white teeth.

'Turn her around now,' Danny says. His voice seems oddly hoarse. Helena's breath feathers against the skin at the top of my thighs. I feel a wave of expectation, but she slowly stands up, wiping away the final drops of water from my stomach, my breasts and throat, leaving me with an ever-mounting sense of frustration. Her arm is warm around my shoulders as we stand, breast to breast, hip to hip, giving the camera smouldering glances as if it is intruding on the intimacy we are sharing.

'Fantastic,' Danny murmurs behind the lens. 'OK, let's take a break, and then we'll do some dressing up.'

I feel too hot and quivery to drink my cappuccino. I don't know what I want precisely from either of them, only for this swollen dam of frustration to break and release me into rapture.

'Do you always get excited by your work?' Helena asks Danny, as our make-up is refreshed.

It's the question I have always wanted to ask, and she comes straight out with it!

'Not always,' he replies, with a cheeky smile.

'Do you go both ways?' she asks.

He smiles over his coffee mug. 'Definitely not. You ask a lot of questions.'

She smiles approvingly. 'I like asking questions. I like to know who I am dealing with.'

'Same here,' I say. 'I too appreciate beautiful things.'

She looks over at me. 'English women. So pink and perfect. Like roses.' She strokes my hair back from my face, and slips her hand into my dressing gown to caress my breast, stroking the nipple with her thumb. Danny's smile falters. Desire fills his eyes. He sets down his coffee cup.

'OK, girls, let's get back to work.'

'He's such a hard taskmaster.' Helena pouts, winking at me.

We are led into another studio, dominated this time by a huge bed. I feel much more comfortable with this. Claret sheets are spread over the mattress. A large gilt mirror hangs on the wall to the side. All the windows have been blacked out and the lighting adjusted to focus on the middle of the room.

Cosying up together on the bed, we are photographed in a variety of tasteful yet suggestive poses. We both know the score, and what the punters like. It is slightly predictable, I think, as he scatters rose petals all over our bodies. Even a little tame.

Apparently, he thinks so too. He takes a few shots of me behind Helena, easing down the straps of her gauzy black teddy to expose one of her breasts, and seems suddenly to tire of the whole process. He puts the camera down.

'Either of you girls object to bondage?'

We look at each other and laugh.

'Bring it on,' I say.

He takes us into his dressing-up room, as he calls it. It's filled with a smorgasbord of costumes from the Regency period on up. There are colourful silk dresses, velvet waistcoats, fancy frock coats and modish pinstripe suits, as well as wigs and hats and shoes, from dainty embroidered pumps to thigh-high white PVC boots. One section holds enough studded black leather collars, tiny latex dresses and snug-fitting catsuits to stock a sex shop.

'Let's give all those nice gents a shock, shall we?' He smiles, clearly relishing the prospect, and to be honest, so am I. As he is characteristically so serious about his work, this is highly unusual for him.

Twenty minutes later, Helena has poured herself into a leather catsuit, and is struggling with the zip at the front. Between us we manage it, although her breasts look as if they have been inflated with a bicycle pump. I kneel on the floor to fasten her boots, which are held together with silver buckles. For some reason I find this act highly arousing. I almost wish she would be a little stern with me, in that accent of hers that is perfectly suited to giving sexy orders. I run my hands up the back of her legs and tremble at the feel of the leather so snugly adhered to her long muscular legs.

Danny has already started to take pictures.

We teeter on evil Perspex platform heels to the studio with the bed. Danny looks us over critically.

'Good,' he says, somewhat dismissively I think. The restricting latex is making me feel hot and even more turned on, especially after spotting the telltale swelling in his trousers. He might act cool, but he cannot fool a keen-eyed woman.

First he has us standing, our arms around each other, giving the camera the old come-on. Then I am fondling Helena, exposing a nipple and giving it a tweak to make it long and huge. Suddenly, I am tempted to take it in my mouth. I swoop down without warning and lick it, curling out my tongue and giving the camera a saucy look.

'What the?' Danny is too surprised to take the picture.

'I couldn't resist it,' I say, grinning. 'Tastes better than champagne, and that's saying something.'

Helena giggles. 'I don't mind if she does it again.'

So I do. In fact, I do it several times because Danny isn't satisfied for various reasons, and by the time he is, Helena is slightly flushed. Her lips go all pouty and her eyes become half-lidded and dreamy looking, but it's Danny's reaction I am most interested in. A flush has appeared on his pale throat, under the fine cotton shirt, and his erection is almost obscenely noticeable.

'Dynamite,' Danny mutters. 'Now get on the rug.'

By the time he has posed Helena on the floor, and me with one foot on her crotch, pointing a small, lethal-looking riding crop at her throat, I know the magazine isn't at the forefront of his mind.

'Is this for the magazine or for you?' Helena asks, again eerily reading my mind.

Danny fiddles with the camera, and doesn't reply.

'You like it like this, Danny?' She growls. Her hand toys with the zip at the top of her cat suit. He isn't taking pictures now. He is following the descent of the silver zip, achingly slow, the leather parting to reveal pale skin while still clinging lovingly to her breasts. The teeth of the zip on each side strain to break apart when the fabric is at its most taut, in the middle of her bust, just before her nipples are freed. They pop out like raspberries, and all the while she is undulating her body, slowly. I am mesmerised, watching Danny, his lower body betraying his every thought. With an effort he snaps out of it and moves hurriedly away, saying something about being back in a moment.

'I think we can be really naughty with that man,' Helena whispers to me. 'Are you interested?'

Of course I am interested! I have been feeling hot and wet since seeing his reaction to our bathtub shoot.

'I'd like to see him beg for mercy,' I reply.

'You English girls are wild,' she says. 'What you say we give Danny a nice surprise this evening?'

For the final shoot of the night we go down to the basement, where he has set up a bar and pool table and used Art Deco furnishings to recreate the look of a retro gin palace. Black-and-white photographs of women in erotic poses dominate the room. The counter itself is black granite, behind which the tiles are mirrored. A row of optics hangs on the wall above it, and a parade of red velvet-upholstered stools line the bar. All around the room, matching red leather couches are pushed against the wall. It seems too permanent to be just there for a shoot. I wonder whether this is his little adventure playground, where the cameras are normally switched off.

Helena has been made up to look like a Hollywood film star of the 1940s, which isn't difficult because she is already stunning. The silk vintage Oscar de la Renta dress fits her like a second skin and shines like quicksilver in the soft light. Even before she puts her make-up on, I know this shot is going to work. Her blonde mane is curled into an elegant, sleek chignon, and her eyes are made up like Garbo, all smoky and soft. Diamonds for her throat and ears, and she looks like a goddess of the silver screen.

I'm more of a Grecian goddess, with my hair combed back and tumbling down in curls down my back. My white gown drapes in liquid folds over one shoulder, while my waist is nipped in by a pretty white corset trimmed with iridescent white feathers around the décolletage. Silk flesh-coloured stockings and high heels strike a subtle contrast to Helena's cool beauty. Historically accurate it wasn't, but I suspect we are now in the middle of Danny's own fantasy.

I suspect it even more when he tells the make-up and

camera assistants he won't be needing them any longer tonight.

He takes a few shots of us individually, striking cool or come-hither poses, the gowns teasingly displaying the tops of our stockings, but it isn't long before he asks Helena to get on the pool table, which she does, striking a sultry pose with a white fox-fur stole. The camera lovingly records her slender curves, the smouldering eyes and Jean Harlow lips, half-parted in desire for the man behind the lens. Helena is flushed, her nipples distended against the silk of her dress. Underneath, she wears a filmy all-in-one with slender straps and French knickers. At Danny's command I peel the dress away to reveal it, oyster-coloured and exquisite, hardly hiding her nipples, which have been darkened with rouge.

Helena mutters something in German and arches her back in invitation. The camera snaps, and I ravish Helena's beautiful breasts, leaving a gleam of lip gloss on her flesh, following Danny's command. Just knowing he is watching sends a flush creeping across my breasts. I look over and see Danny, his camera lowered, his jaw slack. It seems he cannot believe what he has brought to life.

'Come over,' I whisper, almost before I'm aware I have spoken. Woodenly he complies, and his hands reach out for ours. In his weakened state, Helena and I manage to get him on the large green baize table, Helena grabbing his shirt and pulling him over her. As he falls on her breasts and neck like a starving man I walk around the table, issuing commands as he has previously done, before reaching underneath for his zip. He moans and nearly collapses on Helena at the unexpectedness of my hand cupping and squeezing him. I manage to unzip his jeans so he can fall, hot, heavy and unencumbered by underwear, into my hand. I guide him towards Helena's hot, slick centre, and the camera records the ecstatic expression on their faces as he slides inside her.

'No shots. Just watch,' he pants, moving slowly. Helena is muttering guttural words in German, her eyes wild as she hangs on to the table. Danny's eyes are on me as he begins to plunder her body for real. I stand in front of him and slowly peel away my dress, letting it fall to the floor to reveal the white, iridescent-feathered corset. It is so tight that in my highly aroused state my breath comes in little gasps, accentuating the fullness of my breasts as I lean towards him. With a delicate little shimmy I emphasise their creamy temptation, inches away from his hungry lips.

It looks as if he is going to lose it but he struggles off the table, leaving Helena a whimpering, wilted mess, her hands frantic between her legs to give herself the orgasm he has cruelly denied her. He comes up behind me, pressing himself between my buttocks as he toys with my breasts, popping out my nipples from the shallow cups so that the stiff feathers will stimulate them even more. I kick my gown away and stand just in the stockings and the corset, bending from the hip to emphasise the length of my legs as I take him in my mouth. Helena is writhing on the table, her focus fading as she comes, watching me pleasure him as he stands, legs arrogantly spread, watching us both.

As she recovers he picks up his camera again, leaving his jeans unbuttoned as he continues the shoot, while we watch him hungrily like caged lionesses, both eager to get our claws into that delicious piece of meat. 'Get to the bar,' he says roughly. 'Helena, you sit on the counter.'

Obediently she does so, letting her silver silk gown fall to the floor. As if in a dream, I follow, sitting on the bar stool directly in front of her. Without being asked, I run my hands up her thighs. She smiles and spreads her legs, leaning back on her elbows on the bar. By this time her hair has come loose and is again hanging down her back, wild and free.

Danny appears at my side, whispering, 'You know what I want. I dare you to do it.'

I stare boldly at him from between Helena's spread legs. 'You know what *I* want, so go do it,' I say. Without waiting for his response I lick a loving trail up along Helena's inner thigh.

'*Mein Gott*,' she murmurs as I do it to the other one. '*Das ist gut*.' Her sex is pale and pink, moist from her recent climax, and Hollywood waxed, coyly peeping out from underneath the tissue-paper-thin material of her lingerie.

'Do it,' Danny whispers hotly, and I can feel him hard against me, easing me off the stool so he can stand directly behind me. Crushed between him and the counter, I am very aware of his hands, hard on my hips, and another, more insistent pressure, against my buttocks.

Helena tastes good, but I hardly notice her cries of pleasure as my whole mind is centred on Danny's fingers, fumbling with the hooks and eyes of my corset, and the desperation to have me exposed to his touch. Helena is shifting ecstatically around on the granite, holding me against her so I cannot protest even if I want to. I am vulnerable, needy, yearning for release from the building lust I have been fighting all day. Danny's finger salaciously probes into my sex, finding the spot I cherish most and stroking it to singing, swelling life. I can feel cool air against my bare buttocks, but only until Danny covers me again with his body, his long, strong thighs tensing against my own. As I feel a searing rod of heat push into me, Helena comes hard. The air hums with German obscenities, her inner muscles suck at my tongue as an oyster sucks in nourishing food.

Danny is a man who likes to take his time. This is no frantic, heated coupling, taken quickly and impulsively, even though I can smell his exertions and see the moisture glistening on his forehead in the mirror opposite us. Over and over he eases into me, building my need. Helena jumps off the counter and presses her naked body into Danny's while I cling on to the cool granite and beg him to go harder and faster. He loses it with a hard cry, and as I look back I can see Helena's sly face close over my shoulder. She is doing something to him that has made him orgasm so suddenly. In the mirror nearest us I can see her hand, buried between his buttocks. She licks her glossy Cupid's-bow lips at me and snakes her tongue out to lick his ear, at which point he utters one long, drawn-out grunt and sags against me, totally wrung dry.

'It's a pity none of that is on camera,' she whispers, as he regains his breath.

He lets his head fall back against her shoulder. He is smiling but seems too exhausted to reply.

Helena moves away so I can escape the hard granite countertop to collapse on one of the couches. It is warm in the room, but I leave my stockings on and slip Danny's white cotton shirt on instead. Danny goes behind the bar and begins to mix Manhattans.

'An appropriate end to a very successful shoot,' he says, putting three olives on sticks and plopping them in three cocktail glasses. He brings them over to the couch and goes to fetch honey-roasted cashew nuts and other small nibbles on a square white china dish.

'Anyone want to watch a movie?'

Somehow, I know it isn't going to be *The Little Mermaid*.

'Don't look so nervous, it's nothing you haven't seen before,' he continues. He goes over to the opposite wall and pulls down a projector screen. 'This might take a couple of minutes. Bear with me.'

Helena stretches her arm casually around my shoulders. 'That isn't your first time with a woman.'

I smile at her. 'No. I like variety in my diet.'

She laughs huskily. 'I think we shall work together again. Maybe in Germany, or New York. They would love you in New York.'

I'm thinking, I would love New York as well, but my attention is now on the screen. Danny comes back and sits down between us, and we curl up together. I recognise myself on the screen, suave and sophisticated. There are three images, all taken simultaneously by three cameras at different angles. Helena comes into shot. She looks cool and beautiful, indifferent, yet we have the pleasure of knowing otherwise. Even though I realise what is coming, I still hold my breath as Danny makes the adjustments to my costume. I haven't realised until then just how fit he is from the back, his shoulders broad and shapely, his backside as hard as iron. She toys with the close-clipped hair at the nape of Danny's neck and reaches over to stroke my face. We are silenced by the beauty of what we see on the screen. Knowing what is about to happen only increases our anticipation.

'This is a good movie,' Helena says softly. 'What do you plan to call it?'

Danny looks at me. 'Any suggestions?'

I think for a moment, and smile. '*For Our Eyes Only*.'

5

If You Can't Stand the Heat

'You with the hair, smarten yourself up!' These are the first words Guy Le Noir says to me on my first day at Rouge et Noir, a small, painfully exclusive restaurant in St Germain des Prés. I think back to my interview with the sous chef, Alain, who warned me then about Guy's moods, and I swiftly tuck a stray lock of blonde hair under my neat white cap and go back to what I'm doing.

I feel out of my depth among the giant utensils and cold sharp lines of the kitchen – boxed into a stainless-steel arena where the pressure is steaming and the competition is gladiatorial. It's a zero-tolerance zone for error; even less for dithering. I'm imagining army discipline and regimental, boot-camp tactics. Running a Michelin-starred restaurant kitchen is akin to waging a military campaign – daily – so Guy has said in his many interviews. It's evident he has no time for anything less than one thousand per cent effort.

In various parts of the kitchen, keen members of staff are getting on with their tasks. I am feeling conspicuous: my uniform is a size too small and, until a replacement is organised, it is all I have to wear. The others all wear T-shirts under long white zip-up tunics and black cotton trousers, but mine is too snug for that, so I have taken the T-shirt off and am wearing just the tunic and my underwear.

I'm busy peeling fennel when Guy notices me.

'Hands, girl! Are you a student or what?' He stabs a finger at the washbasin by the fire door. 'Use liquid soap.'

Annoyed and humiliated at this second reproach in less than thirty seconds, I go to wash my hands. Alain speaks quietly to him as I dry them, and then they both approach me. Alain introduces us, presumably to stop Guy addressing me as 'girl', and he grunts some sort of acknowledgement. He is good-looking in a slightly weathered but distinguished way, with his own thick, black hair tucked under the regulation white cap.

'Not bad certificates,' he says, with reluctance, referring to my CV.

'Thank you.' I just about refrain from saying 'sir', although it seems to fit. His powerfully built frame exudes an air of reined-in energy.

'So live up to them,' he says, and turns away. Alain gives me an 'I did warn you' look and follows behind him. Chris, one of the more senior chefs, grins at me over his bubbling pan of potatoes.

'I think he likes you,' he says.

'Great,' I mutter, acknowledging the irony.

Some days it's worse than others. Those are the days when he hasn't been laid the night before, Chris says knowledgeably. As I watch Guy handling a delicate maple sugar basket with hands like shovels and a frowned expression of total concentration, I ponder just how interesting a concept his sexuality could be. I reckon a man like Guy Le Noir doesn't 'just get laid', unless the woman is an Amazon. I can imagine his apartment, the neighbours fleeing the building: 'Le Noir's getting his rocks off! Take cover!'

I'm grinning to myself at this scenario when his shadow falls over me in the kitchen. He's been in my face for days, pouncing on every small mistake I might make before I've actually made it. And when he's not telling me off, he's watching me. I'm definitely in his sights. My *Poire Belle Hélène* went in the bin, and today he's reacted to my butternut-squash velouté like I tried to poison him. There was nothing wrong with it; even Chris said so. Guy's just being bloody-minded.

'Do it again,' he says in a kind of growl. 'Too much nutmeg. It must be smooth. Silky. A savoury kiss.' He stops me as I turn away and I can feel his gaze boring into my lower back. 'Let me tell you a little thing,' he says, with heavily contrived patience. 'When people come to this restaurant they want the food to ravish them, not bully them.' His eyes glitter. 'You do know what I mean when I say ravish? Huh?'

'Oh yes,' I reply, trying to be perky. 'I've just never heard it used about vegetables before.'

His intense stare moves up and down my body, which reacts as it always does when a fine male specimen shows interest. I can feel myself becoming hot and turned on, and my nipples spring to attention. And I know he's noticed.

'Maybe, I think, you have led a sheltered life,' he says softly, teasing. When he says think, he pronounces it sink, which I find ever so sexy despite smarting from his constant criticism

'Don't bet on it.' I heft another butternut squash in my palm and boldly wink at him. Immediately I turn back to what I'm doing, suddenly too shy to look him in the eye without going as purple as the cabbage that's accompanying today's Scandinavian-themed entrées.

My velouté meets with everyone's approval, and I know I have gotten under Guy's skin. All in all, it has been my best day yet. And that night, I cannot resist thinking about him in a sexual way, including the inappropriate uses of root vegetables. But by the end of the week I am ready to put his head in a blender. The atmosphere in the kitchen is fraught. Everyone has been seared by his criticism. And we all anticipate it getting worse.

'His girlfriend has savaged him,' Chris whispers to me behind a stack of pots and sieves and *bains-marie*. 'Last time they ... you know ... broke the bed. Now she's told him to calm down or beat it.'

'How do you know all this?' I whisper back.

'She's my girlfriend's sister.' He grins and clenches a fist in a suggestive pose. 'From Marseille. Tough girl.'

We beat eggs and shred smoked haddock and chop herbs together, brother and sister in arms.

'What do you mean, calm down?' I hiss under my breath, eager to know all the details.

'You know.' He gives a subtle thrusting motion with his hips. 'I hear he's a bit of a tiger. Animal, you know.'

The thought electrifies me. So that's where his aggression comes from. He's driven by primal urges. A predator. A meat eater. Top of his food chain. Conscious of his eyes on me, I quickly look and see him turn away. He must have been watching us. Maybe he heard. Maybe his animal senses can detect my aroused flesh. My odour. My longing for such masculinity.

The next day, he is worse than ever. The staff keep out of his way, and avoids his eyes, which is especially difficult in the confined space by the prep area. When I get a moment, I peek into the restaurant. We've all got our work cut out – it's full with fashionable diners gesticulating to their clients and lovers, keen to show off their indulgent, discriminating taste in restaurants. These people have high expectations. They like impressing and being impressed. The décor – at least – delivers. Guy Le Noir has personally chosen it all, from the duck-egg blue walls to the dark leather sofas and smoked-glass tables, covered in cream linen at night for more intimate dining. The muted lighting is hidden behind panels in the walls, which hold paintings in soft, complementary colours.

The sound of my name being called sees me spring back to the clatter, hiss, sizzle and steam.

'You need to get your breasts out,' says Chris, grinning as usual.

'That joke's getting kind of tired,' I say as I retrieve my poussin from cold storage. It is wonderfully cool in the giant refrigeration room after the humidity of the kitchen. I lean back against the wall and sigh. There is no one else about so I unzip the front of my tunic to release the heat. At once my nipples stiffen and feel acutely tender under my fingers. I toy with them, indulging my erotic thoughts about Guy. My other hand drifts downwards. Slips into my panties. This won't take long, I think. I'm so easily aroused here, in the presence of powerful but restrained sexual appetite. Time ceases to have meaning as I idly play with my nipples. Flashes of Guy appear in my imagination. Tied to a large bed – his body hard, his eyes hungry – he curses me for taunting him, for refusing the release he craves ...

Startled by a sudden noise, I open my eyes. Gasp with surprise. Guy stands just inside the door. There is disbelief and desire set on his face, as he takes in my open tunic, and my breasts pushing out of a red-and-white polka-dot bra. In the time it takes to ruin a baked Alaska, my surprise turns to hideous embarrassment.

'What the hell?' He approaches me, eyes transfixed by the tanned flesh on show. He reaches out with those powerful hands. But instead of seizing handfuls of abundant softness, he zips up my tunic.

'Back in the kitchen.' His voice is more a hiss than a whisper. He can hardly talk, let alone blink. I rush past him, back up the stairs. Leaving him to stare at my tight buttocks, bouncing away as he tries to get his breath back.

* * *

Every man has his weaknesses, and Guy needs hard sex with the object of his desire. Tearing a beautifully prepared feast apart with his bare hands; gorging himself and then sucking his fingers clean. And, unlike his girlfriend, the thought of this powerful appetite makes me more attracted to the idea of being eaten alive than ever before.

Later that evening, I feel extremely wicked and choose a red, uplifting satin bra and tiny panties to match. The bra cups push my breasts together, creating a succulent cleavage that my chef's tunic can only enhance, with the zipper slightly lower than I have previously worn it. One tug and someone might get a quivering handful.

Steady on, I think, slightly breathless and feeling a little damp. But I can't help it. Even when he is bawling me out for something I haven't done, the sheer masculine force he displays turns my tummy over and then braises it.

'What are you doing now?' he demands, making me jump. I can feel his breath ruffling my hair above my left ear.

'Chopping lettuce,' I reply, calmly.

'Lettuce? Fucking *lettuce*? This is the organic lollo rosso, picked this morning from the earth. Only rabbits and models eat lettuce!'

'Actually, too much lettuce is bad for rabbits,' I say casually. 'It contains arsenic, and there isn't enough fibre in it to be good for their teeth.'

He stares at me incredulously. 'Why are you talking to me about rabbits!'

'You started it.' I go back to my work. Another head of lollo rosso, plucked from the bosom of Mother Earth, succumbs to my ferocious attention.

The knife is snatched from my hands.

'For God's sake, this is no fish. You're supposed to slice it, not gut it. Let me show you.' His long arms surround my body, trapping me against the work surface. He returns the knife to me and then covers my hands with his own. His touch is surprisingly light, but I can feel the potential for great strength in those scrubbed fingers and smooth palms. Together we part the glossy leaves. The heat of his big frame passes into me. Such close and intimate contact with the restrained power of his muscular limbs makes me shiver. And from his position, he must be able to see inside my tunic, down and into my shadowy and fragrant bosom.

'This is one job where you take your time. You never bruise the leaves.' His breath caresses my cheek. 'Let the knife slip between the folds. See. It will find its own way through.'

Rather like the heavy lump trying to nudge its way through his white tunic. He pauses, apparently unconcerned that his natural enthusiasm is so obvious. I shift deliberately, in a movement that may be an answering caress or an attempt to escape. Interpretation is up to him. He pauses a moment longer, our bodies communicating without the interference of speech or too much thought, before moving away, muttering something about 'Rabbits.'

Minutes later the temporary peace is shattered as one of my colleagues is treated to an ear bashing. Too much salt has been added to the sautéed cabbage.

I am more aware of him than at any time before. His clean, fruity aftershave, the sweat breaking out on his brow, the way he can fire instructions whilst pressing together delicate ravioli parcels. Since catching me in the cold room he seems to be drawn to me. The kitchen seems somehow smaller, judging by the way he has to stand so close to me, making me aware of his muscular thighs and sinewy tanned arms, softly furred with dark hair.

The steam from sauté pans and the ferociously boiling water in other vessels billows around, making it hard to see from one end of the kitchen to the other. The pressure to get each dish absolutely perfect every time makes perspiration trickle down the back of my neck – and every crease feels clammy and uncomfortable. There is no time to escape to my favourite place – the refrigeration room – to cool off.

Towards the end of the night, on impulse while changing out of my sweaty tunic, I take my panties off. Even though they are a minimalist scrap of red satin, once they are off, my nether regions feel wonderfully cool and liberated. As I am contemplating where to put them I hear the door open, so I shove them in the pocket of the next overall hanging on the rail. Guy moves past me on the way to the cloakroom, his tunic soaked in red wine, his face like a general after losing a battle. He snatches up the clean overall next to mine and I suck in my breath. Then smile.

When I return to the kitchen the steam hits me like the blast from a furnace, and the hissing, spitting and the clanging of steel pans makes it sound like the devil is making dinner in Paris. Guy returns wearing a clean tunic and begins flipping filet mignon, the sweat beading his forehead, his strong jaw clenched with concentration. Every few seconds he raps out instructions to his crew, including me, with the speed of a machine gun, and mops his brow with a handkerchief he keeps in a pocket of his tunic.

As the evening approaches its climax, he is getting more bad-tempered. He pads down his tunic and trousers, looking for his handkerchief, then snaps something out of the side pocket to wipe his brow again. I see a flash of vermillion silk and flinch.

Oh shit!

I hold my breath, but he thrusts his hand in his pocket again, unaware he has actually used my delicate panties to mop his brow. I look around. No one else has noticed either. Maybe it wasn't such a good idea. I feel cold despite the thick, blanketing heat in the kitchen. There is no way I could get them away from him without being noticed. He is not the kind of man you could pickpocket. What the hell is he going to do when he finds out?

I try to concentrate. The crispy-duck salad is delivered to the hatch, but I'm hardly aware of what I'm doing. All I can think of is Guy's reaction when he finds out what he has been using to wipe his face. Gradually I'm aware of a different atmosphere around the kitchen. The others have noticed, and are exchanging grins and nudges. Chris is barely able to contain himself. There are only two women working in the kitchen, but Julie isn't a pink, frothy kind of girl, so he will presume I'm involved somehow. All evening I wait for the explosion. What is Guy going to do to me when he finds out?

As the last order is fulfilled and borne away Guy sags against the steel work surface and mutters, 'Thank Christ for that.' He delves in his pocket, draws out the damp scrap of material and, for the first time, sees what he's been using. I cringe in the corner as Guy holds up the panties and looks disbelievingly at them. I could strangle Chris, who looks straight at me and grins, instantly pinpointing me as the culprit. Guy slowly follows his gaze. He advances on me, his hand balled into a tightly clenched fist, my poor panties crumpled within.

'Is this some kind of joke?' He looks ready to ignite. The grins hovering on the faces of the kitchen crew are wiped away.

'They're not mine,' I say, in a thin, unconvincing tone of voice.

'We'll soon find out.' His voice is ominously quiet. He looks down at my tummy and nods. 'Show me.'

I look around the room. Surely he isn't going to make me raise my skirt in front of everyone? He doesn't move. Alain doesn't move. Nor does Chris, the great useless lump. In fact, if they were sitting down they'd be on the edge of their seats.

'Do it,' he says, his voice ominously calm. I have no choice. I slowly gather up the sides of the tunic, revealing my thighs, pause, and turn around. There is silence as my bottom, naked and pert, is revealed. I bend slightly, emphasising the length of my legs and the curve of my cheeks. If they are going to look, they might as well enjoy it. I look back at Guy, who seems to be making absolutely sure I'm not wearing any knickers, judging by his frown of concentration.

'Is this normal to take off your underwear in the middle of a shift?' A speaking grizzly bear would sound like that.

'No! They were damp and ...' No, that sounds terrible. 'I mean, they got wet ...' I'm not making it any better for myself.

His eyes are smiling now, shining with a relish in my humiliation and shame. He drops the panties at my feet. 'Go and put them on.'

I scramble for my soggy knickers.

'You are close to a spanking,' he says quietly as I stand to face him again.

'So are you,' I mutter, my face burning with shame. 'With a wooden spoon.'

On Friday evening I'm scrubbing mussels and pulling off the beards, listening to him going through the night's guest list with the restaurant manager. Most of the clientele are business people, but there is a smattering of media types too. He snorts derisively at the names of one C-list celebrity couple on the list.

'Why the hell are they coming here? They live on fucking pizza!'

'It's his birthday,' the manager says calmly.

'Oh well, at least they will be easy to please.' Guy scans the list. 'Who the hell is this Monsieur Depeche?' And then, 'Oh fuck!' I hear him say the name of a well-known food critic, who has formerly been very rude about Guy's culinary skills. Henri de Laroche is a professional gourmet, whose acerbic comments cultivate fury in the trade. Guy has refused to ever serve him again, but if he is a guest of Monsieur Depeche – one of France's coolest designers – there isn't a lot he can do. In the past he has invariably described Guy's food as 'overworked' and 'fussy', and has referred to him dismissively as less a chef than a 'silk-purse merchant'.

The atmosphere in the kitchen is volatile. The most popular meal is medallions of steak with deep-fried red-onion rings and fat fries with asparagus hollandaise on the side. Whenever the deep-fat fryers are on, it means the temperature goes through the roof. We have all changed our whites several times by the end of the evening and Guy, aware of the man sitting outside just waiting for him to slip up, is unbearable.

'She left him,' Chris murmurs when he isn't looking.

'Couldn't stand the pace?'

'Something like that.'

I look over at Guy. Poor lamb. Smile to myself.

Guy also seems to take great exception to the presence of the C-list couple, who are cosying up to each other on one of the gargantuan leather sofas, indifferent with self-importance.

'*Mon Dieu*, look at that. Here, in my place. Get them a room, someone,' he grumbles. And later, 'I can't believe they've ordered a Riesling to go with filet mignon. Maybe next week I put kebabs on the menu. Jesus, they waste my time. It breaks my heart.' And so on.

I've been waiting to seek revenge on Guy for humiliating me a few days before, and this evening's situation serves up the perfect opportunity. As the two entrées for Henri and his designer friend arrive, I sprinkle a little cayenne pepper over each steak while no one is looking.

I no longer care if I have a job on Monday. It wouldn't be so bad to be dismissed by the great Guy Le Noir. Plenty of his understudies have gone on to better things.

With that liberating thought in mind, I set about teasing Guy to distraction, squeezing past him, my hands on his hips, leaning over him to reach utensils. He catches me once in the locker room, changing my tunic. I pull the tab down, just enough for him to see I'm wearing a very wicked quarter-cup, leopard-print bra, before asking coolly, 'Do you mind?'

The desire to rip the tunic away and throw me down on the floor is plain to see, but he retreats again into the insanity of the kitchen, with only a vivid memory to sustain the heat inside his inner kitchen.

As the evening draws to a close he eventually dismisses Alain and a couple of the others, leaving me and Chris to clear up while he busies himself doing things which really could have waited until the following day. Henri and his friend are enjoying coffee. The C-list couple disappeared earlier.

Guy eventually goes out to talk to Henri, and it all seems oddly convivial. Finally, only I am left, cleaning work surfaces for the following day. People in the restaurant are lingering over coffee and cheese. The waiters look dead on their feet, but are still obliging. Eventually Guy comes back in.

'I want a word with you.'

This is it. P45 time.

'I know what you did with the pepper. You think I'm stupid?'

I stand my ground, stay quiet.

'It's just as well the other couple ordered the same. I told Philippe to give them Henri's order. Maybe it's why they left so soon. Quite frankly, I don't care if they think my food tastes like shit. After all, what would they know?'

'You shouldn't have embarrassed me in front of the boys. It serves you right,' I say defiantly.

'You shouldn't have put your knickers in my pocket.'

'I didn't know it was yours. Anyway, the punishment far outweighed the crime.'

When he takes a step closer, I pick up a wooden spoon.

'What are you going to do with that? Huh?'

'Whup your arse if I have a chance.'

He laughs, loudly and with real mirth. 'You would not dare!'

'I presume you're just about to sack me, so why don't you bend over and find out?'

For a moment, it doesn't seem he will, but eventually he

leans against the work surface. 'Go on, do your best. Then it's my turn.'

I slip the wooden spoon between his knees and move it slowly upwards. He tenses, unsure about the sensation. As I trail the spoon up the crevice of his buttocks he jolts slightly, and when I tap him he laughs, with relief. 'Is that it?'

I smack his bottom with the spoon. Harder this time. He raises an eyebrow. Purses his lips. 'Better.' So he likes a little rough stuff. I must have pushed a button when I suggested it before. I hit him again. Then get closer to him, reach around the bulge in his trousers and unzip him. Give him another hard smack, and something flops forward, into my waiting hand.

'What have we here?' I say playfully, testing the length of his arousal. 'Guy's a real man after all.'

He glares at me, moving away from my hand.

'You see, I've had my doubts. Began to wonder whether you saved all of your passion for food.' I smile at him – a direct challenge in the curve of my glossy lips.

'My turn.' He reaches for me. Seizes me by the waist. And I am suddenly sitting on the cold steel surface with his mouth crushed against mine. Forcing my legs apart, he stands between them, grasping my buttocks and pulling me forcefully against him. As he tears his mouth away he glares into my eyes. 'You can be such a bitch,' he says, and licks my face from jaw to eyebrow.

I am stunned, for a moment unable to respond. Grasping the zipper on my tunic, he tugs it downwards, exposing my breasts in their wicked quarter-cup bra. He dives between them, his face possessed with lust, his fingers still digging into my buttocks. He bites me, but I can sense him restraining a much deeper desire to devour me completely. I run my fingers through his hair and tug it, forcing him to face me.

'Does this mean I still have a job?'

'What do you think?' His voice is ragged. He is desperate

to get back to my breasts. I hold him away, waiting for an answer.

'Yes,' he says, unfastening my bra. 'God, these . . . breasts, they've been tormenting me. I see them in my dreams. Do you think I could let them go?' His tongue curls around my nipple with surprising finesse, considering his desperation. I bite my lip and let him lick at the other. My excitement builds with every delicate stroke.

'You taste good.'

I shrug off the uniform completely and push the tunic from his shoulders. He's wearing a tight white T-shirt underneath. Toned and broad, his chest stretches its damp and stained fabric taut. But the scent does nothing but drive me crazy. I want to feel him hard inside me. The restaurant ceases to exist for either of us. We're oblivious to the customers and staff, only moments away on the other side of the swing door. He flips me over like a piece of juicy steak. The cold steel makes my nipples sing. One strong hand lands on the small of my back, the other tears my panties down. The elastic breaks and snaps against my thigh. Dragged back across the smooth steel, he then spins me around to face him again.

'Feel this,' he pants, as he plunges into me. I can feel it. Boy, can I! Even though I've been ready during three weeks of foreplay. His teeth are bared, his topaz eyes focused like a hungry puma with a slender deer in its jaws.

I'm a mess, my hair all over my face, my tits half in and half out of my leopard-skin bra. He pauses after the first deep thrust. We glare at each other for a moment before he plunges in again, even harder. Leaving me breathless, almost choking on the sensation.

Licking my skin, biting me with his rough mouth and sharp teeth, he grumbles at me. 'You smell divine,' he says. 'God, you taste good. I knew you would.'

I stretch my thighs wider, raise my legs higher; invite him in. Pride, dignity, coyness, restraint, reason – they all desert me and I surrender to his assertive but masterly skill. I hold him there by the hair as the orgasm hits – swelling waves of pleasure that make me croak. Panting and red-faced, he thrusts through my high; he is relentless, not permitting me to come down.

'Greedy minx. On your knees.'

Too weak and aroused to argue, I do as I'm told, my panties now dangling from one ankle, and crouch down like a dog, looking back as he rears up behind me on the slippery floor.

'Yeah, just like that. You knew I was an animal. And you teased it. Stuck your fingers through the bars. Huh? Could not resist it. Well, now it's out. And unless somebody shoots him, he won't stop until his belly is full.' And he's inside me again. Fingers pressed deep into the softness of my hips, his manhood jabbing in and out – deep, hard, mounting a female like we're in the wild. At the same time he slaps my backside, urges me on, until his words become incoherent.

'Oh Jesus, this is it!' His tempo increases, almost forcing me under the sink. I look back at him, narrow my eyes and lick my lips. It sends him crazy. Crazier. He thrusts faster, harder. My whole body shakes. I come again, biting my fingers to stifle a scream of sheer animal delight. Then he freezes, his back bowed, eyes closed. And we clench and pulse together.

'Damn, that was good!'

After Guy has caught his breath, he kisses my cheek and stares deeply into my eyes for a while. Then collects his clothes and begins to put himself together. Through the steam and heat of the many kinds of cuisine prepared in this space, his kingdom, he watches me as he tucks himself in and sweeps his hair back into place. Smiles at me. I smile back from the place he has loved me so thoroughly. 'Make sure you give that work surface a good clean before you go,' he says.

6

Arms of the Law

It's a warm summer evening, with a prolonged cocktail lunch behind me plus drinks with my agent and some magazine people to celebrate my success at winning a new contract. I have to admit I'm tottering slightly as I step into the glare of the street outside the cavernous dark wine bar near my agent's office in central London. I'm high with excitement and the prospect of a weekend of fun and no financial worries for the next six months.

As I walk back to the office to collect my bicycle (yes, I do believe it's the best way to get around London if you're brave) there's a rumble of thunder. The sky is darker than it had been when I went into the wine bar, and there's a smell of summer rain in the air. The skimpy slip dress I had changed into for the afternoon drinks party isn't really suitable for riding in, but as I'd bought it on a whim from a South Molton Street shop in an afterglow of Capirinhas earlier that day, I'm damned well going to wear it, rain or no rain.

'What the hell,' I think, slinging my small shoulder bag over one handlebar and kicking up the right pedal with my bronze Carvela strappy sandal.

I refuse to admit I'm wobbling. It's the shoes. No, it's the dress, which hadn't seemed so short when I was perched on a bar stool. Now I feel like one of the Cheeky Girls, for real. The traffic is heavy as I weave my way through it and it's a challenge not to collide with the film-industry runners darting about from Dean Street to Wardour Street or gay men picking up the pace to Old Compton Street before their Dries van Noten T-shirts get a drenching. No one is paying attention to cyclists, although a rogue white-van man calls out something obscene to me, but I give him a cheerful wave, before veering dangerously and grabbing the handle again to keep my course.

Good thing I'm not far from home. I don't want to get soaked either. I fancy curling up with a Chinese takeaway and a movie, preferably something historical and epic with lots of fabulous costumes, and I'll be all set for the weekend. Feeling deliriously happy as I whizz down St Martin's Lane and into Trafalgar Square, where I pull on the brakes a little and begin to sing 'Let Me Entertain You' to myself, although Robbie Williams wouldn't have thanked me for it.

I don't notice the police car until it draws up alongside me. And I don't realise he intends to talk to me until the window lowers. Even then, I think he's passing the time of day and I smile at him, expecting a little banter. How pleasant, and great for public relations. We are both held at the traffic lights.

'Are you having a nice time?' he asks. I don't like his tone much. It sounds rather sarcastic.

'The sun is out. It's Friday evening. Aren't you having a nice time?' I throw back at him.

'I'm not paid to have a nice time when I'm on duty.'

Oh dear. I've copped a jobsworth. I can't see his eyes. They're hidden by expensive-looking blue-tinted sunglasses. They should look naff, but just look super-cool on him. I try not to giggle as I notice the label says POLICE. He's trying to give it the tough American cop pose. But he isn't eating a doughnut, and his accent puts him well inside the M25. Mid to late thirties, close-cropped dark hair, a strong arm leaning on the windowsill of the car. I think he's cute, even though his expression is humourless.

'Why the long face? Am I in some kind of trouble?' I ask, pushing my luck. It hasn't occurred to me until now, but policemen don't usually chat up scantily dressed blondes on bicycles unless either they, or the blondes, are being very naughty.

He's stern. 'Miss, I'd like you to pull over after the traffic lights and get off that bicycle.'

I do as I'm told. I can play chastised very well. And I do like being told what to do. But I also feel a little sulky, and something else builds inside me when I realise the potential for this situation.

'Now step away from the bike,' he says. He's not in the mood for any of my nonsense. Meekly I obey as he parks the police car next to the kerb. He unfolds his impressively large frame from the car seat, and his body just keeps on coming. Six foot three at least, I reckon, though with three Manhattans and the same number of margaritas inside me, I guess my judgement might be impaired.

'Gosh, you're big,' I say, squinting up at him. Against the sun, his silhouette looks daunting.

'Have you been drinking today, miss?' he asks.

He makes me feel about ten years old, about to be told off something rotten. Which, to be honest, is a fair appraisal of his suspect: I do like to feel naughty and be naughty in the most unexpected places. And right now the temptation to be very wicked indeed is becoming irresistible, if only to get a reaction out of this stone-faced man. 'Maybe one or two, and that was at lunch time,' I say, tacking on the last bit hurriedly.

He nods. Patient, relaxed, in no hurry and not at all accusing. 'Did you realise you were riding in a provocative and reckless manner?'

'Provocative?' I glance down at my dress. It had slipped down, revealing more of my cleavage than I intended but, it has to be said, I've revealed more before. Though maybe not on a bicycle. But at least I have decent underwear on – pink, lacy and cut high.

'I mean at the back,' he says, a hint of exasperation tightening his voice.

I'd noticed a light breeze feathering against my buttocks earlier, but ignored it – the dress is gossamer thin, after all. I twist round. The skirt no longer meets the bottom of my cheeks. When I sat down it must have ridden up, showing anyone on my tail a flash of thigh.

'Whoops,' I say, hurriedly adjusting my dress. 'Is that better?'

'Only if you want to cause pile-ups, prangs and cardiac arrest,' he says, raising an eyebrow. 'Now, I'd like you to blow into this.' He produces a breathalyser.

Mortified, I think he can't be serious. It must be one of those ancient English by-laws: drunk in charge of a bicycle. For heaven's sake, hasn't he got more important targets to meet? My high spirits face a sudden plummet once everything hangs on this one small breath. This was one blow job I really might regret.

I pucker up and breathe into the tube.

He watches the numbers go up, and up. Passers-by are rubbernecking and the storm clouds are gathering apace. I hold my breath. Finally he compresses his lips and whips off his shades. He stares intently at me with cool, grey eyes.

'Mmm. Just under the limit, but the way you were riding was still erratic and hazardous, so I'd like you to accompany me down to the station.'

He throws open the back door and motions for me to get in.

'Great,' I say, more on a breath in case he presumes it is a protest. This is really inconvenient, especially as I've got a post-drink raging appetite and, although I feel myself sliding into a petulant sulk, perversely his professional manner and official tone are only making him more appealing. Even so, I don't want to argue or flirt in case it makes my situation worse. The vision of my peaceful evening, my dinner and my plasma-screen entertainment is receding. God knows how long this is all going to take. I've heard about the mountains of paperwork the police have to account for these days. Sheepish, I look around; being recognised while getting apprehended is the last thing I want.

He gets into the driver's seat and starts the engine. The dashboard is bristling with radios and displays and he fiddles with some paperwork before driving off into the traffic heading down past Charing Cross Station.

'I thought when you arrested someone you're supposed to read me my rights and all that?' I pipe up from the back seat.

For the first time there is a glimmer of amusement in his eyes. 'Is that what you want to hear?'

This response unnerves me slightly. I can feel myself getting juicy. 'You are a real policeman, aren't you?'

'As opposed to what – a bank clerk in fancy dress?' He hands me his identity card, which identifies him as one Max Fielding. Strangely, he looks more personable on the tiny photograph than he does in real life. He is actually smiling, for a start. Or is it a cruel grin? Either way, he looks good, with straight white teeth, good jaw definition and sharp cheekbones.

'Very handsome,' I say, handing the card back to him. I turn around to take a final glance back at my bike, now chained to a railing. I bet it won't be there in the morning. And on the handle, my precious Yves St Laurent shoulder bag.

'Wait, I forgot my handbag!' I squeal.

He steps on the brake.

'Stay there. If you run for it, I will arrest you for real.' He goes back for the bag and drops it in my lap. 'What have you got in there, anyway? A brick?'

'It's top secret,' I say. 'I could tell you, but then I'd have to kill you.'

Oh, I think I'm so funny, especially when I'm drunk. But I'm not drunk. I'm just under the limit. The little machine has vindicated me. Though it didn't explain why I'm sitting in this cocoon of black leather, watching his tanned arm as he steers the car through the narrow streets. Every few minutes the radio sputters and crackles with static voices but he ignores it. The silence is as thick as molasses between us. It's the strangest journey I have ever taken.

'What am I going to have to do?' I ask.

'Fill out some paperwork. And answer a few questions.'

'Walk in a straight line?'

'If you like. Maybe you can do the alphabet backwards for me. Any other requests?'

'You tell me.' I'm sobering up fast. I can't even remember being drunk now. Maybe a little tipsy. So is he just teasing me or teaching me a lesson?

'What would happen if I made a run for it?' I ask.

'From a moving vehicle? Those shoes are way too impractical to try anything like that. Or, for that matter, anything else, like riding a bicycle on a city street. And if we were stationary? You wouldn't get far. About ten feet,' he says, lazily, turning around for a second and flashing me his smiling eyes. 'But an attempt to evade an officer of the law? Well. Let me see. I'd have no choice but to cuff you and put you in lock-down to cool off.'

'Handcuffs? It's almost worth doing it,' I say. I like handcuffs. Come to think of it, I like stern, good-looking men in uniform as well. Crisp white shirts, smart dark trousers, black leather belts and polished black leather shoes. They push all of my buttons. Couple uniforms and an air of authority with shiny handcuffs and I can't resist thinking of the potential for some serious fun. But then Officer Fielding just has to upend a bucket of cold water over the pictures forming in my little head.

'It wouldn't be in your best interests, right about now. You'd be facing a charge for resisting arrest, as well as one for disorderly behaviour. And I'd be tempted to toss in another for indecent exposure.'

' There's nothing indecent about the way I'm dressed!'

'Isn't there?' He gives me a sly, sideways glance. 'That's a matter for the correct authorities to decide. Ask me, I wish more suspects would dress like you. Would take out some of the routine. Don't you think, miss?'

'So why did you really stop me?'

'Because you were going all over the road. You could have hurt yourself.'

'That's very considerate of you. But now I'm facing a felony charge. I might lose my job,' I protest.

'I doubt that very much.' His voice is so soft, with an underlying implication that makes the interior of the car seem like our own private zone of sexual tension. Strip away the formalities, and I'm alone with a strange man in a car, after all. I'm beginning to wonder if he's picked me up for his own, distinctly unprofessional reasons.

I shift on the seat, making the leather creak and can feel a luxurious heat through my flimsy dress. My thoughts begin to drift again when I look at the handcuffs attached to his belt and I wonder how much I'd enjoy being restrained like a real criminal – his criminal. Is he doing this for kicks, or have I got it all wrong and he's really a consummate professional who never mixes business with pleasure?

I prefer to suspect the first scenario. In fact, I even like the reverse of the image: him strapped to a chair, hands cuffed behind his back, while I parade around and tease him until he's hard enough to burst. I'd give him a lap Dance, asking him, 'Is this indecent? Or this?' And with every negative answer I would reveal more of myself, until he was straining and demanding to be set free so he could rip the last few wisps right off me before manhandling me over the interview table.

We stop suddenly. My fantasy has completely transported me out of the car. We're downtown already – in a car park, facing a brick wall.

He opens my door, and waits for me to peel myself off the seat. I have to do it carefully, as I'm stuck to the leather. I hope I haven't left a mark. Glancing back, I see the perfect imprint of two pert buttocks indenting the leather, but nothing more.

We go through the glass double doors into the police station.

At the desk, a curt and buxom woman in uniform glances at us and gives me a 'not another one' look. Turning around, I can see why. Three girls, a little younger than me, have already been brought in. One of them is sporting a black eye. Looks like there's been a catfight fuelled by alcopops. They're still hissing and sniping at each other when I'm led down a corridor to a room near the end. As I round the corner, I hear the policewoman bellow 'Shut it!' at them in a tone Vin Diesel would find hard to ignore.

'This is where we'll make absolutely sure how many drinks you had at lunchtime,' PC Fielding says.

'Surely it doesn't matter when I had them. I'm either over the limit or I'm not,' I reply.

He looks at me, a slight smile on his lips. 'Maybe you'd like to think real hard and remember?'

'I didn't have many. I told you.' I'm hotly indignant. Or maybe it was my pants catching fire.

'Are you sure? Are you telling me you were on orange juice all the time you were in Joey's tonight?'

My jaw goes slack. He must have followed me, all the way from the wine bar back to my agent's office and on from there, which definitely isn't normal procedure, but how else would he have known I was going to get my bike?'

'You told your friends you were riding home. I could see you were … the worse for wear, so I decided to make sure you were safe,' he says, as my realisation I'd been staked out becomes obvious.

'Isn't that taking your duty to protect the public a bit too far?'

'Do you wish to make a complaint?'

'Damned right I do! You've been ...' I grope for the word and can't find it, '... very sneaky!'

He laughs lightly. 'Ouch. Is that it, or do you wish to make it official?'

He's watching me closely. Under the flickers of the strip lighting he is a rigid colossus, towering over me with a handsome face of angles and shadows. No, I don't want to make a complaint. I want to punish him personally. Preferably with his own night stick. Then I want him to ... I glance at the table. There it is, with an unappealing orange plastic chair on either side. Even so, grey Formica has never looked quite so tempting before.

'You know what I really want to do?' I say heatedly.

'Enlighten me,' he says dryly, perhaps expecting me to throw a tantrum.

'I want to lay you out over the table so I can spank you raw. Does that count as disorderly behaviour?'

If he is shocked by my confession, he makes a good job of hiding it. His eyes narrow. 'That depends if there are witnesses. Otherwise it's my word against yours. You wouldn't have a leg to stand on.'

'Neither would you, by the time I finished.'

He raises one eyebrow. 'Threatening behaviour now? You're running up quite a rap sheet.'

'Oh, bugger off!' I slump down on a chair and fold my arms across my chest. It's so tempting to hit him, I'm afraid I might actually do it.

He says nothing as he strolls to the door. After he shuts it behind him, I hear the metallic clunk of a lock being turned.

Great, so now I'm in a grey room with three pieces of furniture and not even a six-month-old magazine to look at.

On one wall there's a large, long window, but it's filled with mirrored glass, which is weird. Did my misbehaviour warrant observation from other officers, or are all the other interview rooms filled with skimpily dressed, tipsy vixens?

Officer Fielding comes back with a cup of coffee for himself, and a paper cup of water for me. 'You need to rehydrate,' he says, putting it on the table.

'Would it be possible to use the ladies first?' I ask.

'Sure. Come on.' He leads me back out to reception and calls WPC Cleaver over. Her magnificent bosom arrives before she does. She gives me a terse look and tells me to follow her to the toilet. More banging of doors. There is not an ounce of soft, fluffy comfort anywhere in this place – it's all right angles and hard surfaces. Especially in the toilet stalls.

When I'm escorted back to the interview room, Officer Fielding is in conference with another man, who gives me a loaded glance before disappearing down the corridor. He isn't too hard on the eye either. I get a thrill from being in such close proximity to all this power and paraphernalia. Officer Fielding locks the door again and motions for me to sit on one of the chairs, taking the other one. He spins it around and straddles it. The casualness of the action only makes it more sexy.

'So, what am I being charged with? I know how it goes. You have to charge me or release me.'

'You're not going to be charged. You are under the limit, but only just.'

'So I don't have to walk the line, do the alphabet thing, stand on my head?'

'You can stand on your head if you wish.'

'I don't think so. You've seen my knickers once already today.'

'Yes, I have.' He says this with the utmost conviction and folds his arms over the top of the chair. They're smooth and sinewy under his short-sleeved shirt.

'Off the record, they were very pretty,' he continues. 'And as for what's inside them, I bet that's pretty impressive too. But I still have to give you an official warning, and then escort you home. To make sure you don't get back on that bike again today.'

I'm flattered by all the attention, but disappointed too. I'm still expecting something a little more exciting than a reprimand. The handcuffs, the uniforms, the authority, the thrill of being in trouble have all combined, got inside my head and made me ready to misbehave.

As if he could read my mind, he removes the handcuffs from his belt. He lets them dangle from his index finger. Swings them gently, as if suggesting their potential.

'You have been a bad girl,' he says, his voice soft, but commanding. 'In a way, that may not fit within the parameters of the law. And perhaps you still need something to remind you of exactly how inappropriate your behaviour has been. I mean, these days, the roads are filled with hazards. And motorists just can't afford to take their eyes off the road for a minute, can they now, miss? So how many drivers do you think you distracted tonight and sent home in a spin because you couldn't be bothered to dress appropriately for riding a bike? And I won't even mention the lack of a helmet. Then there's the poor control of a two-wheeled vehicle on a public highway. Chalk it up with being uncooperative, and attempted bribery and corruption – trying to charm a police officer out of his uniform. Just like those motorists, how do you think I'm going to sleep tonight?'

'I've heard that masturbation is very good,' I suggest coolly.

Lithe and silent, he rises from the chair and approaches me. He clips one cuff around my wrist and the other around his. Speechless, I do nothing, just watch him. Treating my silence as compliance, he draws me to a standing position, using the cuffs to lead me. He sits on my chair, and pulls on the cuffs so I have to face him.

'Sit on the table,' he commands. His husky voice is taut with the authority of a genuine command. I feel the hard edge of the table brush against my buttocks as I move into position. It feels cool as I slide on to it. Slowly, he reclines my body back until I'm lying down. My nipples spring alive as I feel the cold, hard surface of the tabletop against my back. I remember I need to take a breath and exhale before I go dizzy.

Events are taking a surreal turn, especially when he unlocks the cuffs about his wrist and clips them around the top of the table leg. From his utility belt, he produces a second pair of cuffs and fixes my other arm to the furniture. My heartbeat quickens. My skin gooses. But I feel compelled to surrender control to Officer Fielding.

'Now, where was I?' he asks, before drawing the night stick from its scabbard. He's obviously relishing his role, milking it for every effect. Maybe I should be afraid, but I know instinctively he has no intention of harming me. It appears we are both indulging compatible fantasies – he picks up a sexy girl, restrains her, then chastises her; I'm a girl who wants to be picked up, restrained and chastised. The weekend is starting to have more promising aspects to it than a takeaway and a movie.

The blunt tip of the stick moves down my body – the contact gentle, but invasive. I feel its stubborn pressure between my breasts, over my tummy, going down towards my legs. Then it pauses … and lifts the hem of my dress.

When it nudges against the cleft between my legs, I stretch like a waking cat in a pool of sunlight. Though I long for a more assertive push from that blunt instrument, I crave an even more assertive push from something else – Officer Fielding. And he knows it. His smile is teasing as he steps away and walks around the table, tapping the stick against the edge while he patrols my disgraceful display.

'But I'm not convinced, miss, that you'll take any notice of a conventional warning,' he continues.

The stick taps, taps, marking his presence around the table, around my head and speeding pulse. He stops at the end where my feet are.

'Look at you. How could something so damned sexy be anything but a bad girl? You're bad to the bone, miss. So what kind of deterrent should I choose to prevent you from reoffending? It'll have to be something special. Mmm? Something unique. Tailored to your exact requirements and circumstances.'

Subtly, he glances at the one-way glass and fights a smile.

And in a heartbeat I know we are being watched. Behind the glass, an unknown number of men and possibly women are observing the interrogation. A powerful shiver frosts my spine. My legs turn to water.

'Set me free,' I say. 'And I'll show you how good I can be. I'll show you all.'

'Is that so?' He runs the night stick up between my legs. I shudder, but yearn even more intensely for a different kind of rigidity.

'Is that all you got, Officer? Maybe it's the only thing that's hard in here.'

He shakes his head. 'You got a lot of spunk, you know that?'

I wriggle seductively on the table. 'I could do with a top-up.'

He smiles again, but only with his eyes. Slowly, he runs a hand up my leg, teasing, stroking the softness of my pampered skin. I don't want to fool around any more. I want action, a hard response, zero tolerance, and lots of it.

He pushes my dress up around my hips, exposing my sweet pink knickers.

'These are just pretty,' he says, playing his fingers over the tiny triangle of silk.

'Maybe they should be kept as evidence.'

I no longer care what happens to my designer panties. His other hand is hot and dry on my stomach, caressing the skin on my hips and waist. He seems to delight in its golden softness, but he is also consciously prolonging my frustration, until it becomes a torment. Just as I am about to tell him to speed up the process, he swoops down and traces a faint line across my stomach with the tip of his tongue. Writhing in its tingling wake, I lift my buttocks and push my sex at his mouth.

When I feel his hot, moist breath on my most intimate place I gasp and squirm, helpless. What are they thinking behind the glass? As I feel his tongue play with me I imagine them – stern-faced men in uniform with massive erections, their steely eyes fixed on the pretty, sexily presented evidence being invaded by one of their lucky colleagues. Maybe the buxom woman is in there too, going down on them one by one. I hope so. The image is so powerful, I feel myself sliding into glorious abandon. Moaning with delight, I open myself wide so he can investigate me at will.

I'm squirming and grinding my silky bottom around on the table while his mouth does a patrol around my pussy. Using his lips and teeth and tongue, he moves all around me. I can feel the whole of his mouth on my sex; the strong wedge of his chin and the grit of his strong jaw against the soft skin of my inner thighs. Thorough, eager, hungrily, his beautiful masculine mouth feasts between my legs until I have to bite my bottom lip to stop myself crying out and confessing every misdeed of my adult life. By the time he stands up and unclips my steel bindings from the furniture, I'm so red and dizzy with pleasure, I'll sign any confession he puts in front of me.

Effortlessly, he picks me up and carries me over to the glass. I can see our dark reflection as he sets me down, his arms locked around my body. Hot, damp kisses pepper my throat and neck. Clenched teeth pull the shoulder strap of my dress down my arms. Long supple fingers are thorough in their interrogation of my trembling, willing flesh – exposing and teasing out my nipples, delving inside my panties to stroke and flick and press in all the right places – and all the time, his hard leather belt rubs against my tender skin. A stubborn thickness pushes into the small of my back while I'm pressed up against the glass – its chill keeps my nipples hard. I can only imagine what is happening on the other side; I think of chiselled faces only inches away from my soft and wanton shape – adoring it, wanting it.

Faint with arousal, I fall against Fielding and he leads me back to the table. He sits down on the chair and tugs me after him. I am about to perch on his lap but he straightens my hips and pushes my knees apart. I know what he wants. The penal bracelets around my wrists tinkle as I twine my arms around his neck. With my back to the wall, I sink down on his lap and wrap my legs around the chair. Instantly, I can feel something thick and hard between us. Feels like his night stick, though not quite as long. It's his any time of day or night stick, I think, while falling deep into the cold but beautiful grey waters of his eyes.

He gathers up my dress to expose my bottom to the observers. I lean back until my hair brushes the linoleum, giving them a good view of my breasts falling out of my dress. Fielding's fingers tug at my nipples to make them even thicker. His breath is no longer even but heavy and laboured. He must be desperate for release. He's already making a superhuman effort to continue with more of this foreplay. I sit up and press harder against him, allowing him to feel my heat and eagerness through his trousers.

'Time to set you free,' I whisper, reaching for his zip. 'I think you've been punished enough.'

I am seized by the upper arms, spread over the table and held down. A chair falls on its side. I feel vulnerable, yet still eager to accept whatever he chooses to do to me. Fielding stands between my legs. His fingers work fast to unbuckle, unzip and release. Then his large shape is over me, on me. A thick tongue snakes out and licks each of my prominent nipples. He just helps himself to the prisoner. His strong, broad hands run all over my curves and intimate parts until I am writhing beneath his weight, responding to every sensation, be it hard or gentle. Too much sensation. I'm overwhelmed. And Fielding just devours me – all afternoon his desire has been building for the cheeky minx riding the push-bike all over the road, and now it has found release.

'Who's behind the glass,' I mutter, wanting even more stimulation.

'Colleagues.'

'How many?'

'Four.'

I nearly pass out. Behind that sheet of thin glass, four thick erections are pointing at my body – all so eager to indulge themselves as well. I imagine strong hands vigorously working away while they watch their colleague getting physical with his perfumed 'perp' in a sealed room. Officer Fielding is right – I'm bad to the bone.

Desperate to be taken, I wiggle into position so he is forced to take me, deep and thoroughly.

Reading my signals, understanding my need, he gently raises his body and pulls my hips closer to the table's edge. Slips my high-heeled feet on to his shoulders. Kisses my ankles. Licks my toes. Then slips inside me.

He feels huge. It forces me to cry out. He pushes slowly at first before building to a savage tempo that leaves me wordless, then breathless. I clutch at the table, fearing it will collapse under our aggressive coupling, but am too engaged in every jolt and shudder and thrust of this crazy ride to mutter a warning. Soon, our combined cries are resounding around the closed room. Mine get higher as I get higher, rising to my peak faster than ever.

Officer Fielding groans. Holds my wrists tight. Kisses me brutally. I see the animal in his eyes and drop over the edge into a climax so intense I want to pass out, cry and laugh all at the same time. I feel one strong pulse inside me before my arresting officer pulls out and shoots me at close range.

Breathing like he's chased a felon across a mile of uneven ground, he then stares down with satisfaction at the mess he has made of my new dress. He smiles at me. Winks. Then leans forward and kisses me. And we stay like that – still joined, hot, sweaty, and triumphant. And I can tell this round of questioning isn't over yet. His eyes are still lively and hungry for the sweet, naughty blonde wriggling in his cuffs. Already I'm anticipating a home visit. I mean, he may need to gather more information and run over a few more points he's not clear on. And I anticipate committing future felonies on his beat, which may result in fresh cautions. Oh yes, I'm already looking forward to more protection and service in the strong arms of the law.

7

Sporting Chance

I hear him before I see him. The stream of curses floats through the A&E ward to where I'm making notes on my last patient.

'Don't tell me, that one's mine,' I say to the receptionist standing next to me.

'You got it,' she grins. 'He's been giving us hell ever since he arrived.'

I pick up my clipboard and check my hair in the small mirror on the wall behind the desk. Maybe the sight of a shapely blonde nurse will improve his temper.

'His name's Matt McGregor. Slipped in a tackle and got his head clocked by the toe of a football boot. Passed out briefly, and sustained a nasty cut on the forehead, plus some bruised ribs. Assorted scuffs and scrapes, nothing serious.'

'Lovely. And they call it a gentleman's sport,' I say.

It's just what I need, a grumpy football player with a headache. I brace myself and whip back the curtain. He's smeared from top to toe in mud, blood and grass stains. His shorts were probably white that morning, but it's difficult to tell. The white and red shirt is scuffed with detergent-challenging stains most mothers would give up on. He holds a white gauze pad to the side of his head. One side of his strong, handsome face is covered in drying blood.

'About frigging time,' he says moodily.

The man standing with him, obviously a fellow player and not much cleaner, joins in, grateful to have something useful to do. 'Yeah, we've been here hours.'

I glare at him. 'Because of his head injury, Mr McGregor has been made top priority.'

'That's not saying much, is it,' the man grumbles.

You don't need to be in here, so why don't you come back later?'

They glance at each other, and look more closely at me. It is obvious they expected me to be a pushover. Until now all they've seen is a snug white uniform, blonde hair neatly tied back in a bouncy ponytail, and perky breasts. Being told off isn't part of the equation.

'I'm not going to eat him,' I say. 'Not while he's that filthy, anyway. Go on, hop it. This is supposed to be a clean environment, which it isn't with you dripping mud all over the floor.'

'Er, right,' he says, the wind totally taken out of his sails. 'You call me then. I'll tell Dick what's happening.'

Matt nods. 'Dick's the manager,' he says almost meekly, as if he has to explain. Now he is on his own with me he seems a bit apprehensive.

I look at the notes that the doctor had written.

'So you're being kept in for observation,' I say briskly. 'How are you feeling now?'

He has the most startling pair of tropical blue eyes I have ever seen on a man, and when he uses them to full effect I find myself warming to him. Underneath all that gore is a healthy alpha male struggling to get out.

'A bit pukey, to tell you the truth,' he says, grinning weakly. He has a gentle, winning smile. I'm beginning to like this man very much. There is a familiar pull in my lower regions, especially when I catch him copping a look at my breasts.

'That's understandable. Lie back on the bed.' I smooth the pillow behind him and cover it with a white hospital sheet to protect it against the mud.

'But … I'm filthy.'

'Don't worry about that for now.' I lay my hand on his upper arm, feeling it tense. There are some reasonable muscles under that football shirt, and if they are anything like as toned as those on his thighs and calves then here is a beast not easily tamed. I resist the temptation to run my hand along his bicep and squeeze it, and turn my attention instead to his wound.

It's a relatively simple cut, requiring cleaning up and Steristrips, but because he lost consciousness the doctor has decided to keep him in for observation. I look at the dirt surrounding the lip of the wound and clean it carefully.

'When did you have your last tetanus booster?'

If it's possible for him to turn pale under his mask of blood and mud, I could have sworn he did.

'You mean … a jab?'

'That's what I mean,' I say, matter-of-factly. Inside, I sympathise.

'Well … when I was a kid, I guess. But I don't need one now, do I?' Those green eyes are beseeching. Again I find myself melting under their heat.

'We'll see what the doctor says,' I say briskly, turning away.

Outside, I talk to the ward sister. Even though it's the end of my shift, I am happy to sort him out, clean him up and make sure he is all scrubbed and tidy for his night on the ward. My reasons are not totally altruistic, but she isn't to know that. I go back into the cubicle with my equipment on a trolley and set to work.

'Is it going to hurt?' he asks.

'You'll feel a little discomfort, but no more than you're used to.'

He shuts his eyes and I see his jaw clench as I begin to clean around the wound. Even his toes scrunch up. His eyes are tightly closed, giving me the opportunity to examine his face. He has fine, chiselled features, his short straight hair dark and glossy. Playing in the sun has given him a faint tan, turning his limbs to golden perfection.

'Will I need stitches?' He asks tentatively.

'It won't be necessary. We wouldn't want anything to blemish those good looks, would we?'

He tries to grin, but it hurts. I turn his face towards me and lean over him to apply the Steristrips, one by one. He is close enough to nuzzle me if he wants, but he does not, probably fearing a slap. The Steristrips applied, I give him a soothing stroke on the leg, my fingers aching to squeeze those lean, hard muscles.

'You must think I'm a big pussy,' he mumbles, looking a little flushed.

'I'd be more worried if you'd enjoyed it.' I smile reassuringly at him.

'It wasn't that bad at all,' he grins, giving my breasts a suggestive glance.

'This is the nice bit,' I say, carrying a bowl of water back to the bed. 'You can relax for a while.'

'I can't wait,' he sighs, and relaxes into the pillows.

I begin at the top and work downwards. He lies back and closes his eyes as I wipe the blood and mud away from his face. Although the hospital lights are bright, and there is noise and bustle all around us, our closed-off cubicle seems peaceful and quiet.

'You are a handsome sod under all this, aren't you?' I say cheerfully.

He has the class not to look coy. He was obviously aware of his attractiveness. 'I bet you say that to all your patients.'

I grimace. 'Believe me, I don't.' His beauty is almost feminine, yet his demeanour and hard body make him all man. From his voice I can tell he has been educated privately at some point.

'So what happened?' I ask, taking my time cleaning him up.

'It was bloody slippy out there this afternoon. The rain stopped play in the end, so all this is for nothing.'

'Were you winning?'

'The visitors were idiots, but they were lucky.'

'I'll take that as a no, then.'

He glances carefully up at me, ready with a terse response, but seems to realise he is looking straight up between my breasts, which shuts him up.

'I won't even mention the recent England–Azerbaijan game,' I say mischievously.

He groans loudly. 'At least we won, but we should have slain those bastards. What a – ow!'

'Keep still,' I say firmly, holding his head steady. 'Otherwise I'll Steristrip your mouth shut.'

'You mentioned it first,' he mumbles. As I take my time tending to his cuts and bruises, bad thoughts of undressing him drift through my mind; stripping away those ridiculous long socks to expose well-muscled calves, easing down his shorts to reveal taut, firm buttocks. How would he react if he knew what I was thinking? I often wonder, when tending my more attractive patients, what they would be like in bed. Sometimes, fantasising is all that gets me through the afternoon. Some of them look at me almost thirstily, as if they ache to yet dare not make some sort of pass. I have spent a few interesting evenings after a 'What are you doing later?' or a 'Can I buy you a drink sometime?' Something about the white and blue uniform just does it for some men, just as football shirts and long, lean bodies do it for me.

I shake my salacious thoughts away.

'OK, it's all done, I'll just go see about that tetanus booster.'

'Do you have to?'

I smile at him, rubbing his cheek comfortingly. 'Are you telling me you're afraid of a little prick?'

'Depends where you're planning to stick it,' he mutters. He gives me a hunted look. I walk to the end of the bed and run my hands up his calves.

'I'll tell you what I'm going to do. I want you to be a big, brave boy and have this injection, and I'll give you a nice bed bath to make you all clean and respectable for going up to the ward. Deal?'

After the briefest hesitation, in which I can tell he is wondering whether this service is commonly available on the NHS, he nods. I treat him to a little wiggle in my walk as I leave him to find the doctor.

A few minutes later I am back at his bedside with one of the doctors and a tray containing a needle and swabs. 'Now this usually goes into the top of the thigh but as you still need cleaning up, we can't risk any contamination so that means ...' I pause dramatically, 'We need to get into your shorts.'

'You're enjoying this, aren't you?' he says, as he turns painfully on to his side and pulls up his shorts, displaying a magnificently muscular male buttock.

'I derive immense satisfaction from my job,' I say serenely, trying not to ogle him. It's a good job the doctor is there. It is all I can do not to swoop down and sink my teeth into one of those pale, perfect globes. He glances over his shoulder at me, looking worried. The doctor smacks the area he is intending to invade, leaving me free to enjoy the ripples coursing through his flesh, then swabs and sticks the needle in before he has a chance to think about it.

'Ow! Ow, sonofabitch, ow!' he yells, squirming so much he is in danger of falling off the bed.

'It's over! Calm down!' We hastily put up the sides of the bed to keep him safe and I hold up my two hands, devoid of nasty things meant to cause pain. 'See? Done.'

Matt looks sheepish. 'Didn't feel a thing,' he says. 'My ribs hurt though.'

'You were very brave.' I soothe him, stroking his hand. The doctor gives me an 'oh please!' look and leaves the cubicle.

He is grinning now, flashing startlingly white, straight teeth. 'Bullshit, but do I still get my bath?'

I glance at my watch. 'My shift finished five minutes ago,' I say regretfully. It is gratifying to watch his face crumple in disappointment. I grin at him to show I am not going to let him down. 'But I need the overtime, so why don't I arrange for us to go up to the ward so we can free up this cubicle for the A&E staff? Then I can give you your bath in more privacy?'

'Privacy?' he repeats thickly, blinking at me. I walk my finger up the swell of his hamstring, stroking the back of his knee, and let my hand drift higher to rest on the top of his thigh. He follows its ascent, and swallows visibly when it reaches the top.

'I might even get you into a private room,' I say, my finger tracing a circle on his skin just underneath the hem of the shorts.

'I think I've had a really bad bang to the head,' he says, somewhat huskily.

I lean over the bed, so he can feel the warmth of my body against his arm while I check his dressing.

'It is a very nasty injury,' I say, smiling down at him. My breasts were almost brushing against his broad, muscular chest, but not quite. 'Let me take you upstairs.'

'Now I know I'm dreaming,' he says, and lies back to resign himself to his fate.

While the doctor speaks to him and examines his various sore bits, I prepare a bowl of warm bubbly water, flannels and towels. In the bathroom I tidy my hair, slick on some lip gloss, and ease the skirt of my white uniform up slightly, holding it in place under the elasticised belt with the large buckle at my waist. For good measure I also unfasten the first two buttons of my uniform, affording a tantalising glimpse of creamy skin to anyone inclined to look.

I wheel in the trolley as the doctor goes out, and tell him I will let the ward sister know when I am done so she can set up Matt's observation machine. As she and I are old co-conspirators from our nursing college days, it hasn't taken much to arrange a private room for my man, although her comment was, 'If you get caught, it's not my call.' As it's nearly ten o'clock by the time we arrive there, and the doctors have now completed their rounds for the day, it isn't very likely.

Matt looks surprisingly perky for a man with a head injury. He gives me a frank up-and-down look, taking in the black patent stilettos that I have also changed into, the white stockings, and the short white dress with a cleavage he's sure hasn't been there before. He's right. It hasn't. But thanks to a silky white push-up bra with front-loading fastener, it can be there all night if necessary. However, I doubt it will be too long before that fastener is popped and my best assets are getting total appreciation.

'Let's see what we have here,' I say, gently closing the door and pulling the shutters down. The lights are low and, outside, the city sparkles like a faraway kingdom. At night, the impersonal grey rooms take on an intimate life of their own, depending on the patients' wishes.

I ease the white socks down his legs, revealing calves as shapely and firm as I had expected. The hair on his legs is as golden as that on his head, and silky to the touch. I run my hands up his legs and back down, and again he shivers.

'Cold?' I asked.

He wordlessly shakes his head.

'You're very tense.'

'I'm sure you'll be able to do something about that.' His voice shakes slightly. He is watching intently as I wash the dirt away from his legs, lifting each in turn and bending it at the knee to get at the underside before drying them with a soft towel. My adjusted uniform eases tightly over my breasts and accentuates my backside as I stretch and bend, lifting each limb with competent hands. He is as compliant as a drugged dog, yet I sense an air of expectation, and know that if he is inclined to get up and take control, he probably could.

'Shirt next, and you'll have to help me with this.' He lets me unfasten the buttons and help him to a sitting position so he can gather the shirt up and slip it over his head. I haven't appreciated fully how impressive this man is until I see the well-defined muscles on his smooth chest.

'Wow, someone works out,' I comment casually. His stomach is as flat and hard as an ironing board.

'You like that, do you? A man who spends a bit of time on himself?' I swear his chest swells with pride. He is very proud of his body, rather like I am with mine.

'Most definitely. What do you like?'

'Is it true what they say about nurses, or just a cliché?'

'I have no idea what you mean,' I say primly. As I help him lie back down I realise he could take over right now. This doesn't alarm me. In fact, it turns me on even more, for I am the one in charge. He is the one waiting, needing the touch of the hot flannel and my small, soothing hands. He watches me unwaveringly as I wash the dirt from his neck, his arms, and for good measure, although it is totally gratuitous, his chest and stomach.

'Don't want you complaining I didn't do a thorough job,' I say, smiling at him.

'There'll be no complaints from me,' he replies. He closes his eyes and lifts his face as I swab the mud and blood away. His nostrils flare at my scent, floating up from somewhere beneath my breasts. It is L'Eau d'Issey by Issey Miyake, and not too much. I hadn't wanted to scare him, or get him thinking he has no control over what is happening.

'So it is true,' he says softly, his eyes still closed.

'What's that?' I pat his face dry, and as I inspect his wound again I let him feel my body, warm and curvy in the snug uniform, brush against his chest. His hand, gentle and sneaky, brushes against my cotton-covered backside.

'What they say about nurses. It's true. Either that or I'm in the middle of a fucking wonderful dream.'

'It's all in your imagination,' I say, moving away from his light caress. To be honest, it could have been his imagination, until then. Apart from a couple of risqué hand movements I have done nothing inappropriate whatsoever.

'Now it's up to you, but I'm very happy to wash your groin area.'

I am half expecting him to whip his shorts off faster than a bride's nightie, but instead he smiles.

'Go ahead.'

'But first, I'd like you to turn over.'

He looks crushed, but isn't about to protest. It takes a couple of goes, owing to his tender ribs, but he gets there.

'Comfortable?'

'Yeah,' he says breathlessly. He adjusts his position, as if there is some obstacle he is trying to remove from under his lower body. 'Yes, I am now.'

'It won't take long.' I wash him with long strokes, down his spine, and towel him dry. He lifts himself up so I can get the shorts past his buttocks. They join the other filthy garments in the bin bag on the floor.

'Can I offer a massage to relieve some of that tension around your shoulders?' I ask.

'Offer anything you like,' he replies, muffled into his pillow.

From my pocket I produce a small tube of jasmine massage oil. I warm some in my hands and spread them over his shoulders. His skin glistens under the grey lighting as my hands slip effortlessly over his upper back. He groans with pleasure as my fingers circle and probe, hunting out those elusive knots of tension. It is awkward working by his side, so I climb up on to the bed and sit astride him, my body lightly resting on his. He moans even louder as he feels my weight on his legs.

'Does that hurt?'

He can't seem to answer. Eventually he shakes his head. He seems to have gone into shock. All the tension is back, but my magic fingers gradually melt it away. Shuffling down the bed, I concentrate on his buttocks, really getting into squeezing and digging into those delicious pale globes. His body shifts until it feels as if I am sitting on the bottom of a small boat. He is moving with me, pushing his hips into the bed, his breath catching in his throat.

'Oh, this is good,' he mutters as I move further down, fingering around his inner thighs and the crease beneath his buttocks. He wants to spread his legs, but my legs straddling his won't allow him to. Cruelly I deny him and watch him amorously rubbing against his mattress instead.

'You can turn over now,' I say eventually. I kneel up to let him shift around. At first he doesn't.

'Give me a minute,' he gasps, a little flushed in the face.

'Come on, don't be shy.' I pat his lovely pert bottom. 'I've seen it all before, you know.'

'I'm sure you have but ...' He doesn't know what else to say, so he turns over and reveals himself to my hungry gaze.

He doesn't look relaxed at all after his massage. In fact, he looks as if he has run a hundred-metre race. The bulge at his groin sticks out further than Henry VIII's codpiece, and I find myself wondering what the hell is in there?

'Wow, that's some packet,' I say, giving it a little tweak. It gives slightly under my fingers and springs vigorously back, making me jump. Way above, Matt is smirking at the way I had snatched my hand back, like an outraged virgin. I ignore him, pouring the by now grey water down the sink and filling the bowl again, humming softly to myself. I take my time and he waits. This time the water is much hotter, but pleasant against his skin as I concentrate on his lower stomach and upper thighs, only just avoiding the area he is hoping I will eventually reach. After a while I decide it is time to take the bull by the ... horn. Never before have I been intimidated by designer elastic and I'm not about to start now. I take up a pair of wicked steel scissors and brandish them.

'Snip, snip,' I say, smiling mischievously. Matt's smirk disappears. He looks afraid for his prized possession. Carefully I tackle the thick elastic at each side. The sound of cutting material is loud in the quiet room. Matt watches me as I peel the garment away, waiting for my reaction.

I do my best not to betray my delight, but I am impressed.

'I don't think I really want to share that with anyone else,' I say evenly, crawling up the bed to sit astride him once more, this time covering his modesty. There is a slow, insistent beat, reverberating through my body. Matt is now walking his fingers up my thighs, to the hem of my dress. His eyes rest at the vee at the top. My skirt has risen to reveal my stocking tops and a shadow of what lies further up. Holding his beautiful sapphire gaze I reach behind to unfasten my hair. The movement strains the buttons of my uniform over my breasts even more and it is my turn to gasp as he flips one button open just as I manage to free my hair. It falls soft and shiny and fragrant around my face as his spade-like hands cover my buttocks, treating them to the same appreciative caresses as I've been giving his.

He lets his hands roam, over my breasts, down to my neat waist, flaring out to the curve of my hips, fingers digging in, questing. I move against him slowly, a seductive movement that teases and stimulates every nerve ending in his lower body. My body moves to the insistent, instinctive rhythm, aware of his innate desire to lift, to thrust, but even the taut muscles in his legs are not enough to allow him to take over. Helplessly he has to let me tease him to distraction, while his fingers confidently conquer the remainder of my buttons. He yanks the uniform aside and manages to pull himself up enough so he can bury his face deep into my breasts, groaning like a man in a trance of ecstasy. I can feel his breath, his stubble scraping against my tender skin, but most of all I can feel his tongue, long and probing, lapping up the essence of my skin, my female fragrance, while long arms of iron wrap themselves around me, rendering me unable to move. I shudder hard when a fingertip pulls down my bra and his tongue darts around my nipple. Latching on to it, he gives me exquisite sensations, and it is my turn to squirm and grind myself on him. I always wondered if I could orgasm just by having my nipples teased. If it is ever likely to happen, then now's a good time. I am consumed with rapture and delight at having this man under my control.

Finally I can stand it no longer. Reaching underneath our bodies, I pull my panties aside and, without ceremony, grab him and guide him into my heated body. He falls back, too shocked to cry out, his eyes feverish, his teeth gritted in concentration. He can't move much because of his ribs, so I do it for him, gently rising and falling with a steady tempo that leaves us both breathless with arousal. His hands go into overdrive, trying to feel every bit of my body at once. A past master in stifling my cries of pleasure in tricky situations, I clap my hand over his mouth and ride him harder, feeling his hard thighs tensing under my own, my mind working overtime at the thought of how good he would be at the height of his power, when he could use the full weight of his body to push against mine – maybe somewhere near the football pitch, in the bushes after a Sunday game when all the others are in the showers.

His eyes are fixed on mine. I can imagine the things he's saying silently in his head; the dirty language he wants to use but daren't, in case I leave him high and dry. We climb to breathless, almost silent ecstasy, made more intense by the danger of someone walking in. He is making tiny but concentrated movements with his hips, and I know he's close. Then he lets out a muffled roar, hot and moist against my fingers.

A couple more pushes and I am there also, my breath fanning his face.

He holds me tight for a few more moments of intimacy before kissing me and letting me go. I slide off him and, tidying myself up, allow myself to gloat over my conquest. His chest is still heaving with exertion. The flush of arousal has stained his cheeks and neck.

'Do you give this kind of service to all your patients?' he asks, somewhat croakily. His fingers are stealthily gathering up the hem of my skirt and tugging on my suspenders.

'Hardly ever,' I say, making him decent and snug with a crisp cotton sheet. I plump his pillows to make him comfortable, reluctant to leave him. Our breathy coupling hasn't been quite enough for me. I have only experienced a fraction of this man's potential. It makes me feel weak just to imagine what he would be like at full strength.

'I'm hungry,' he says, letting the suspender snap back against my flesh.

'I don't recommend the food,' I reply jauntily, knowing that insipid mushroom soup is the last thing on his mind. Almost unbelievably, he has begun to swell under the sheet again. As I palm the telltale bulge the door opens, and two men walk in.

They are tall and muscular – other football players come to see how their team-mate is bearing up. They take one look at me and realise he's doing pretty well, thank you very much. There are knowing smiles, coarse laughter. I don't mind. They are pretty easy on the eye, just like Matt. I smooth my uniform down over my hips and try to look professional, even though I feel anything but.

'I was just about to eat,' Matt says to his friends, motioning to me. They look my way, uncertain exactly what he means. I know exactly what he is getting at. This time I make sure the door is locked before turning back to the men, my fingers on the top button of my uniform.

8

Always the Bridegroom

Jake is a friend of an acquaintance who was married last year. Cruising on the periphery of my ever-shifting circle of friends, he has always been a definite prospect for adult fun, though his potential has never been realised, due to other people getting in the way. But what a real dish – tall, lean and muscular, with boyish good looks, a cheeky smile and a naughty sense of humour. And I almost managed to bag him between the dessert course and the speeches at the acquaintance's wedding. I say almost – a few amorous dances and a lot of tipsy snogging outside the hotel in the dark was all it amounted to. It was a snatched moment of hasty, champagne-fuelled lust, with the real business remaining unfulfilled a year later.

Every time I saw him at a function or party, which wasn't nearly as often as I'd have liked, I'd feel a surge of attraction, but we both needed a hefty push to do something about it.

And then she arrived. The bitch. Dainty and petite, apart from a chest like Lara Croft, which I suspected were the two main reasons Jake was attracted to her. Not that I'm lacking in that department, but she played the vulnerability card, which is something I never do – I like to be a bit more sporting than that. She elbowed her way into our crowd – bust first, the rest following – and wasted no time in claiming the eligible, breast-obsessed Jake as her own.

Strangely, we began to see more of each other. He was welded to her arm every time I joined the crowd for drinks after work. He looked at me over her sleek, poised head, and I knew he was remembering that heated ten minutes in a hotel garden. The way his eyes flickered up and down my body, checking out my tight jeans, my snug low-cut top, told me all I needed to know.

And then I heard the inevitable – he and Donna are getting married in six months. That was hardly a shocker, but when she asks me to be a bridesmaid, I'm floored, then a little anxious.

Why me? At the risk of sounding catty, do I sense a little twist of revenge here? I think she suspected an attraction between her fiancé and me the moment I was introduced to her. So maybe she now wants to demonstrate that I am the loser in the contest for Jake's affections. And it will be churlish, if not downright suspicious, if I refuse the offer to traipse up the aisle behind her, holding the hem of her gown.

But then, people are not always so straightforward in their motives. And Donna is a woman I would never underestimate. For instance, whenever I ended up in the same bar or party with Jake and Donna, not all of the eye contact was necessarily between me and Jake. If I'm not mistaken, I've often caught Donna looking at me in unexpected ways. There might have been some quick, dismissive glances in my direction whenever Jake failed to restrain his enthusiasm at the sight of me in a low cut top, but as an evening progressed I would gradually become aware of her subtle, admiring looks. Twice I caught her looking intently at my legs and bottom, and I'll never forget the time we kissed each other on either cheek in a typical London welcome, and I felt her hand deftly stroke the curves of my bottom. I thought it was an accident, at best a sign of growing affection, but now I'm not so sure.

I don't join in the wedding preparations. It isn't something I'm interested in. But Donna has commissioned a London designer to make our dresses, and I'm quite happy to let her get on with it. She does have good taste, which makes her even more irritating, but at least the final result won't be horrendous. Though again, I can't help but suspect she only wants me to look my best while I'm punished.

Coupled with the odd admiration she seems to have for my figure and the way I present it, this makes me begin to think how events could take a turn towards the erotic. It is often the case that antagonistic dynamics have a sexual undertow. That constant clash of emotion – competition with a begrudging desire – can make us irrational. Can force us to abandon reason in the most unlikely circumstances, and to give in to what lies beneath. So which will win, Donna? The frost of indifference on your beautiful face, or the heat of passion that smoulders below, ever ready to ignite into something fiery and unrestrained?

Donna and I go for the dress fitting three days before the wedding. And I spend more time with her in the week before the wedding than in all the time she's been with Jake. Reluctantly, I am even beginning to warm to her. She has this infectious laugh and a wicked sense of humour that seems to hold no real malice.

'I really hope you like the dress. You'll certainly get noticed,' she says as we walk through the door of an upscale designer shop for my first and final dress fitting.

'Great,' I say, staying chirpy and determined not to go for any of her Donna bait.

But over the last few heady days, filled with girly coffee meetings and talk about shoes and make-up, there is one thing I have forgotten until now. No one, not even top supermodels, *ever* look good in a bridesmaid's dress. And that's the whole point – never upstage the star. Perhaps that's why she's being nice – I'm being patronised by the sympathy of the victor.

Donna's dress is exquisite, in cream satin covered with tiny seed pearls and delicate embroidery, cunningly cut to show off her impressive décolletage. It hugs her curvaceous figure all the way down to the ground with almost obscene devotion, and at the back, the material fits snugly over her shapely bottom, opening into a vent filled with a waterfall of more extravagantly embroidered satin. As well as accentuating her curves, it also enables her to walk elegantly without hobbling. All it needs is a simple string of pearls and her mother's wedding veil, and she looks like a vision. I want to run my hands all over her silky body, and I smile to myself thinking of the reaction I would provoke from the snooty proprietors by such an unexpected and shockingly inappropriate display of aesthetic appreciation.

I shake myself back into reality, stalling my wayward thoughts, and finding myself a little overwhelmed by the emotional charge of the situation. The happy day. I suddenly feel like crying. Donna is getting married and she's going to look like a princess. And I nearly do burst into tears when I see my dress, but for an entirely different reason.

Taffeta has been out since the 80s and, unless I am mistaken, it hasn't returned as a cutting-edge fabric. The smile aches on my face as the bridal consultant unwraps the polythene from the hideous garment. Even she looks aghast. Frowns, tucks her chin in, hoping we can't see her reaction, but I catch her look of mirth mixed with derision in a mirror beside the clothes rack. Donna is delighted.

The material is so stiff it could stand up and walk across the set of a horror film unassisted. All I have to do is step in and be zipped up. I feel a tug as the woman ties the sash into an enormous puffy bow at the back, and then steps back to let me look in the mirror.

The colour scheme for the wedding is a daring one, being pink and gold. It could so easily go horribly wrong in incompetent hands, but Donna has managed to hit just the right note with the embroidered waistcoats for the men and the flowers she has chosen. It shouldn't have worked, but it does.

This doesn't.

The taffeta is gold shot through with pink, so every movement shows either colour, or merges into a less attractive green sludge. The dress, if I could grace it with the title, is strapless, with a sash just underneath the bosom that ties into the monstrous bow at the back. The remainder of the dress is completely plain, with no decoration whatsoever to divert the eye from the horror elsewhere. Even worse, the skirt sticks out like a child's drawing and doesn't even have the decency to cling to any part of my body.

I look like a trifle with a French plait. Or a pregnant geisha. Bride of Frankenstein without the scars. Any six-year-old girl would refuse to wear this dress. In the mirror, I see Donna's triumphant grin.

'You look lovely!' she trills. The designer tries to nod, but can only give me a weak smile. She knows I look like a trannie in a tutu.

'Wow,' I say, with no strength to my voice. Her tactics are foolproof – this tasteless monstrosity will guarantee there is no serious competition on her special day. 'It's …' I struggle for the appropriate word and can't find it. 'Bright.'

'I knew you'd like it!' Donna claps her hands and laughs like Cruella de Ville in a new coat.

The day arrives under a canopy of sky so blue it hurts to look up. Relentless and oppressive, the heat will be sure to turn my tinfoil taffeta enormity into a microwave. The wedding is a typical upper-middle-class affair. The groom, best man and ushers wear black trousers and long-line jackets, with the pink and gold waistcoats and bow ties underneath. Jake looks dashing in a frock coat, jazzy waistcoat and pink cummerbund. There are Jacques Verte and Alexon for the more mature female guests, in all the colours of an English country garden; for the young, a flash of Anna Sui, a wisp of Ghost. The teenagers dazzle in flashes of Morgan and Kookai. Silk wraps drape around bare shoulders for the cooler evening, and St Tropez bronzed legs are everywhere. Everyone is trying to outdo everyone else, but no one will outstrip the bride for sheer beauty. Especially not me.

All through the church service, the guests cool themselves with their hats or with pretty paper fans, given out to the female guests as a last-minute touch. Donna has thought of everything – her complete control is impressive, almost intimidating. I feel sorry for Jake already, imagining daily life with this woman eighteen months on from the honeymoon.

I hold my fragrant sheaves of lilies and gypsophila and vivid pink roses and feel my body temperature rise inside that wretched dress, bitterly envious of the light summer slips and bare legs while mine are basted with perspiration and pink as an English holidaymaker who's spent too long on a Benidorm beach. Following Donna down the aisle I am sure I hear a comment along the lines of 'What does she look like?' Jake has a small double take at the altar, his eyes widening at the sight, not of his stunning bride, but the pink-faced monster whom he used to lust after. I swear I'm going to follow the bitch on her Maldives honeymoon, with a sniper's rifle in my Louis Vuitton suitcase.

The session with the photographer seems endless, and my hair is bedraggled by the end of it, while Donna looks as fresh and elegant as the moment she rose from the beautician's chair. Even her smile is set hard like frosting on a wedding cake. Only when I feel a hand on my backside do I perk up. It isn't Jake's lecherous uncle with the smashed-plum nose, but Jake himself, standing innocently with his bride under a yew tree for the final shot. I tell myself that it must have been my imagination. Surely he isn't about to feel me up in front of his guests. Not when I look like a flashback to the worst fashions of the 1980s.

The afternoon reception is held at a very upmarket hotel on the Thames, and it is during the banquet of oysters and roasted salmon that I have time to assess the surrounding male possibilities. The best man is an amiable idiot, slightly plump, very cute and very married. Bride's father: too old; Jake's father: too boring; a few other males: too attached to their beautiful, keen-eyed girlfriends.

Jake looks hot and uncomfortable. He keeps looking my way, his handsome face unreadable, but he's drinking more champagne than can be good for him. I notice a couple of girls also looking my way and then suppressing giggles. Can't blame them. If I were in their position, I'd be laughing too. No other male, whether they be young, old, bald, fat, ugly or mouth-watering, has looked my way once other than to stare in appalled fascination at the extraterrestrial tent I have bound to my body with a cartoon bow at the back.

In the end, after enduring hours of small talk about their high-flying careers, exotic holidays, the latest Hobbs collection and the best private schools, I have written the day off as a bad deal, comforting myself with the knowledge I'd never see most of these people again. At least the first Dance isn't to 'Love Is All Around'. I doubt if I would have made it to the bathroom in time. Even the one lecherous uncle present – more a tradition than a nuisance – gave up trying to goose my backside, unable to get his liver-spotted paws through bales of taffeta.

As I am about to go upstairs to change into the dress a sympathetic friend had brought for me, Jake appears, holding out his hand.

'Dance with me,' he says. Despite the alcohol I've seen him consume, he's still steady on his feet.

'You won't get near me,' I complain, motioning to the horrid dress. He takes my hand and pulls me to my feet.

'I'll always find a way.' And he does, pressing the small of my back so we are intimately close, his hand holding mine up and out in the classic stance of the waltz. I can't remember the music. Gershwin? Cole Porter? I'm more conscious of his spicy cologne blended with the tang of hot male. His rough cheek grazes mine. His long and lean body presses pleasingly into my curves. 'You look gorgeous.'

I giggle. 'Don't lie. If I put my heart into it, I couldn't look this bad in fancy dress, on Halloween. I feel about as glamorous as a traffic cone.'

'A very desirable traffic cone. One designed to actually stop the traffic,' he murmurs. He glances down to the prominent shelf of my breasts. 'Girl, you'd look good in a paper bag. And I bet they're just dying to be set free.'

'You are a very bad man,' I whisper as we move sinuously together. For the first time that day my self-consciousness melts away. The room could be empty with just the two of us on the Dance floor, hinting with our bodies what we desired to do horizontally.

'I can be very bad,' he replies, with a suggestive shifting of his hips.

'This might be stating the obvious, but I think you're a bit late,' I murmur, held close to his broad, hard chest. He smells divine. I want to rip his clothes away and lick him from head to toe.

'I'm in trouble,' he breathes softly. 'My beautiful wife is over there and all I want ' – he stops, letting his body tell me exactly what it is he wants to do – 'is to be inside you.'

It's as if the contents of a dozen champagne flutes has just gone straight to my head. But I'm unable to respond. Over his shoulder, I see the approach of Donna with a face like a Siamese at a mouse hole.

'Mind if I cut in?' she says to me, leaving Jake no choice but to take his new wife in his arms instead. But how is he going to explain the immense bulge in his trousers, I wonder?

I bustle, rustle and sweep off the dance floor, alone, and feel hot and bothered enough to drag the nearest half-decent man under a table.

As the party moves on to the terrace to bask in the warm evening, I decide to go upstairs to change. Enough is enough. At least one of my torments can end. But Donna slips into the chair next to mine.

'Are you enjoying yourself? You look a little hot.'

My patience is at an end – special day or no special day. 'Are you surprised? Why did you make me wear this dress? It's foul.'

She nods, not looking the least repentant. 'I know. You must hate me. In this heat too. It must be punishing. And I guess it might even work as a kind of chastity belt. To deter the amorous. But,' she says, sweetly, 'your luck might change. I'm sure someone in here has the key.'

I sit on my hands. Smile along with her until her mother unknowingly saves her from a black eye and torn dress by luring her away to mingle. Jake takes her seat.

'What was all that about?' He sounds tense.

'I was telling her how shitty I feel in this dress. She agreed and thought it was damaging my pulling potential.'

His face softened to smile. 'OK, I admit it. You've looked better.'

'Thanks, darling. And I hope you have a long and happy marriage.'

He leans towards me, winks. 'We both know you'd look a hell of a lot better without it on.'

'How?' I shrug. 'And as I said before, it's too late now.'

'Not necessarily.'

Those two words hang between us and refuse to drop. Shall I even entertain the suggestion he's just made, or back away with a smile and kick myself later? As I hesitate, he takes my hand and guides it into his lap. I'm shocked, not at what he has done, but at the size of what he's concealing in there. I reacquaint myself with a memory of Donna's spiteful smile and allow my hand to stroke the swelling. I even give it a little squeeze. He closes his eyes in bliss.

I wink. 'I need to go upstairs to change.'

'You may need help to get out of that ... dress.'
'I just might do. I might even let you help me burn it.'

Upstairs, the corridors are cool, the thick carpet silent under our feet. The wedding suite is enormous, furnished in cream and green, with an aroma of lilies. The furnishings are late Georgian, dominated by an imperious bed with four oak pillars. A large mirror offers a detailed view from the other side of the room. From the tall windows, we can see the terrace and the guests milling about below, clustered in small groups, hats scattered like brightly coloured flowers on the grass. Donna is among them, enjoying the fawning attention.

'As long as she's in sight, we'll be OK,' Jake says. 'Now, let's get you out of that weather balloon. Good Lord. What was she thinking?'

'Narrowing the field, I believe it's called.'

Jake looks sceptical – doesn't want to believe it. He pours champagne into two flutes that are conveniently waiting on a silver tray on the dressing table. There are also chocolates wrapped in silver and pink foil, an empty ice bucket lined with a linen cloth, and three pink roses in a crystal vase.

'Face it, Jake. She's jealous. She knows we had a moment. If I look stupid it makes her feel better. It's a girl thing. Old as time.'

'If you say so,' He says, with a smile. 'I think she's very, very fond of you. Talks about you all the time.' If he's this clueless about the female psyche, then being married to Donna is going to be one hell of a steep learning curve. 'She's full of surprises too, that's for sure.' Naïve as well. I'm tempted to give him some advice about manipulative personalities, but he drops a kiss on my shoulder and pulls the bow apart with a silken hiss. I can't breathe, let alone speak, as he unzips the dress, letting it fall slowly to the floor.

The sheer relief makes me feel light-headed. I stand in the middle of the room, arms outspread, letting the cool breeze from the window waft over me like a gossamer caress.

Underneath, I'm wearing a hot-pink strapless bra with *balconette* cups. My full breasts rest inside, temptingly on display, yet half-hidden. Jake walks around me, kicking the dress out of the way. He takes his time, adoring every inch of me, shedding his clothes as he circles me. The long-line jacket is shrugged carelessly off his shoulders, the waistcoat following. As he unfastens each button, his eyes are on mine, a smile broadening his mouth. Off goes the waistcoat, and he flings it contemptuously away, together with the bow tie and cummerbund. The blonde spikes of his razor-cut hair shine in the sunlight streaming through the windows. Down below, I catch sight of Donna walking down the garden towards the river with her equally frightful mother and another woman, probably an aunt, who looks like a ship in full sail in her swathes of pink voile. Our haven is suggestively quiet and fragrant.

'Once?' he asks softly, for the record.

'This is the bridal suite,' I remind him.

'It's four walls and a shitload of expensive furniture,' he counters. He gives up on the cuff links and leaves his shirt undone instead, baring a sculpted smooth chest and dark-brown nipples. Moving in very close, he kisses the slope between my breasts, douses my curves with his warm breath, his tongue slipping about. His hands are surprisingly light on my waist. Donna is at the riverside, walking along the bank. I melt with pleasure as he finds a nipple, laps it, savours its taste, then sucks it out to its full length, sending eddies of sensation shooting down my body.

'Once,' I agree, more a breath than a word.

The word seems to break something inside him that he has been holding back for months. He pushes me against one of the poles holding up the canopy of the bed, and slips his hands around me and the upright. Holds my arms there, by the wrists, and continues to plant a trail of kisses downwards. I sag against the pole when I feel the warmth and moisture of his mouth press into the vee at the top of my legs.

'Keep watch,' he murmurs, and I do, through eyes half-closed. I am suddenly hungry for that tongue, suddenly desperate to open myself up and let him gorge on my most intimate flesh. Kneeling before me, he looks up, his eyes drugged with arousal. Holding my gaze, he takes the small string of my thong and pulls it down. The absence of the tiny garment exposes me. He moves in again, and I widen my thighs to encourage more of his probing.

Suddenly remembering that I am supposed to be keeping watch, I look towards the window again. No Donna in sight. I look further along the riverbank. No slim column of white.

'I can't see her,' I whisper, though my voice catches as Jake stands up and presses himself against me, his breath wet on the soft skin below my ear. He is grinding himself against me, unrestrained now, letting me feel the force of his need. We both go to unzip him at the same time. I get there first, fumbling desperately to get at him through his black jockey shorts. When I set him free, he falls, warm and heavy against my stomach.

'She'll be down there somewhere,' he mutters, his hands rough on my buttocks, squeezing them. 'God, I want you. You're so sexy ...'

'I think you should be saying that to me,' says a voice from the door.

There is no way we can get out of it. I am practically naked and he is stiff as a hatchet handle. He moves away from me, but makes no attempt to hide himself from her accusing gaze.

She shuts the door, and locks it. The sound is ominous in the heavy silence. Donna moves into the room, the satin rustling softly in her wake.

'You need to make a choice,' she says. Jake starts to speak, but she stops him with an imperious finger. Then, to my total shock, she reaches behind and unzips her dress. It falls to the floor, and for a moment she looks like a goddess, rising from a pool of glossy cream.

From the back, it looks as if she is wearing ordinary thong

panties and a halter bra, but when she turns around, I can see it is an all-in-one. Her breasts are held up with clever invisible wiring, over which delicate chiffon, translucent enough to show her dark, shadowy nipples, covers her breasts like gathered curtains, leaving her front completely exposed. The material joins underneath her body with a slender satin rope, which holds it up at the back. I have never seen anything like it. It is effectively backless, frontless and crotchless, yet manages to still look elegant. It is utterly brilliant.

Donna sees the envy in my eyes. She looks amused. 'You want to try it on?'

I blink in shock. I want to, but I don't want to. It is hardly the time, and there is a strange atmosphere in this cool, beautiful room; one I don't feel easy with, but am disinclined to run from too. Jake obviously isn't going to help me. He's leaning against the dressing table, casually drinking his champagne, looking louche and elegant despite the fact his trousers are open.

Donna takes off the delicate garment and hands it to me. I can smell her perfume, and the tiniest hint of female musk. She is watching me, a hint of challenge in her eyes, and I know I have no choice. The garment is supremely comfortable, despite the candyfloss panties and the strange wiring. My breasts feel light and supported, yet it is almost as if I wear nothing at all. I feel like a high-class call girl, with my all-over St Tropez tan and gold-strapped skyscraper heels. It makes me want to strut, to wiggle, and to have great, wham-banging, noisy sex with a hot man with enough driving energy to launch a space shuttle. I want ... I stop, feeling breathless, wondering what has come over me.

Jake is watching us with an air of expectation. I get the feeling this isn't the first time he and Donna have played this sort of game. Suddenly, I recall all of those discreet, admiring glances and subtle strokes of my bottom, the lingering eye contact ... She wanted me. Just as much as Jake. Possibly even more. And her attempt to humiliate me in the terrible dress was also an attempt to control access to me. To deter others from interfering with what she planned for me. On her wedding night. Even her new husband was used as a bait to get me up here, for the pleasure of his wife, and the keeper of the key to my chastity gown.

She's full of surprises too, that's for sure.

She's very, very fond of you. Talks about you all the time.

Indeed.

'What do you think?' she asks him, cradling me in her arms. One hand is travelling down, heading between my legs. 'Isn't she a beauty.' As it descends Jake's arousal rises visibly. The gentle pressure on my bud makes me bite my lip and he stiffens in response. I am shivering with a strange excitement as Donna moves away from me and palms his erection, while effortlessly pouring more bubbly into his glass with the other hand. I have to admire her panache. She guides his penis into the champagne, then swiftly kneels and sucks the bubbles and wine from him. He looks intoxicated, but with pleasure. I decide to leave them to it, so I take the garment off again and reach for my dress.

'I'll see you later.'

'I said, you need to make a choice,' Donna says. Her head is on Jake's shoulder, and she is fondling him with a smooth, accomplished movement, but her words are directed at me.

I assumed she'd been talking to Jake.

'Stay, or go?' she asks playfully. 'After all, it would be fun, wouldn't it? A good way to end a wonderful day?' She continues to fondle Jake, who watches me over his champagne glass. Donna suddenly swoops, and he briefly closes his eyes at the pleasure of her mouth. This would also be a good time for me to escape, but I don't feel inclined to. My hand is on the door, but my fingers feel too stiff to turn the handle.

Jake mouths one word, 'Stay,' and I have no choice. I let my hand fall, and Donna leaves him and floats over to me.

She guides to the bed and hungrily kisses me – on the mouth, throat, breasts, tummy – while stroking my back and waist with her eager hands. Gently, she then eases me down to the bed and arranges me so that I lie flat. Staring deeply into my eyes, to hold me still with an assertive but lusty look, she sits beside me and rolls her shimmering white stockings down her legs. Carefully, she then takes each of my wrists and ties them to the posts at the bottom of the bed with her stockings. Stroking and kissing my inner thighs, then my knees and calves, she eventually reaches my feet and places them among the pillows. Once I am arranged and secured by the bride, I close my eyes and abandon myself to the gentle press of female lips, as they move again, all over my throat and chest and tummy, followed by a warm tongue, leaving cooling trails of moisture from my breasts to my navel.

A trickle of cool liquid falls from above to splash and sparkle on my tanned bust. Lapped up quickly by the naked bride before any rivulets reach the silk coverlet. More champagne drips on my trimmed pelt below. Jake, standing over us, controls the flow of the champagne, wordlessly, communicating with his eyes and the erection rearing out of his smart trousers. And Donna is let loose on me, with tongue and lips and teeth, nipping gently, lapping hard and kissing noisily. I am stunned at this sudden turn of events, by this revelation at how their relationship truly works. Nothing as predictable as a horny attached man lusting after his ex girlfriends. But a man controlled, and happy to be controlled, by his clever and salacious partner; a beautiful woman quite happy to use her handsome man to bring soft and perfumed delicacies to her bed, for her own pleasure.

Her delicate breath and flicker of tongue make me cry out. I remember the open window, and realise I no longer care. If people hear, they will understand. Or think they do. And soon I am being licked at both ends and my body writhes under each heady sensation. Donna's firm grip on my thighs keeps me spread and open as she kisses my pussy, then tickles me inside with a reaching tongue. Jake teases out my nipples with a light touch, inadvertently moving close enough for me to capture him in my mouth. He hisses loudly at the wet heat of my mouth as I take him deep. And I hold him there as I peak, stifling my cries with his length.

Below, down there, I thrash and buck, grinding myself on Donna, and as I am still coming Jake pulls away and moves down the bed to fill me up. Moves his pretty wife aside and kneels between my thighs. I twist against my silken bindings, not wanting to escape him, but to grab even more pleasure from a deep and driving force. To my astonishment, I watch as both of her pretty, manicured hands guide the bridegroom's length inside me. The delightfully sinful situation, the illicit location, and the paralysingly naughty idea of who I am actually with, push me further into ecstasy. I begin to cry out, until Donna muffles my joyous shrieks by lowering herself to my face.

Smooth and shaven, she tastes salty but instantly familiar, I want to pleasure her even more than she pleasured me. Kneeling across me, she invites Jake to toy with her breasts, and writhes in sympathy with the attentions of my tongue. I hit the spot, earlier than I expect, and hear her own rapture. She cries out unashamedly, riding my eager, hungry face. Her excitement spurs her new husband on, makes him go harder, faster, so the whole bed and canopy is shaking like a carriage on a cobbled lane, until he tenses, slows, and I feel his wooden muscle pulse inside me.

Out there, in the grounds, any guests who are still lucid will realise there is more than one female in the bridal suite – the thought makes me smile. A soaring devilish sense of freedom from all restraint overwhelms me, lifts me up, takes me to heights I'd never experienced before, before I drift downward, feather-light, to settle on the bed once more.

We all lay together, blissed-out and sated. Jake is in the middle, blond hair tousled, his smooth bare chest gleaming with sweat. We stroke him gently, coax him, kiss him, eagerly awaiting his recovery. It's going to be a long and thorough consummation.

'I'm so happy everything worked out. And that you joined us tonight,' Donna whispers to me.

'I have a hunch a lot of planning went into it,' I say with a cheeky smile.

'Well, you know what weddings are like. Every little detail has to be just right. Especially our unusual nuptial agreement. It took some imagination and daring to pull it off, didn't it, darling?' She kisses Jake's cheek.

He moans in agreement.

'Sounds like you two are a perfect match. It's been an honour to have played such a big role on your big day.' I say, with a giggle.

Donna laughs. 'We wouldn't have had it any other way. We were determined to share even the most intimate tradition with you. You've been in our thoughts for some time. But I think you suspected that.'

'Maybe.'

'And it would be nice to think we've started something that might even become a regular occasion.'

'Well, of course we must celebrate the anniversary.'

'At the very least,' Jakes says, and pulls his girls in closer, until three hot mouths meet.

9

A Tonic for the Troops

'Come on, girl, shift your arse! What d'you think you're doing? Having a morning nap?' The fierce Scottish sergeant bawls incessantly in my ear as I slither under the rope netting, feeling the cold mud oozing through my uniform in all the most uncomfortable places. It's under my fingernails, ruining my French manicure, and in my hair, and plastering my T-shirt to my skin. I stay where I am for a moment, watching the brown stuff squelch between my fingers. The other squaddies are long gone, scrambling up the nets like wired-up monkeys. It's all right for them. They don't have breasts. For the first time in my life I curse them as they prevent me from travelling a smooth path under the clinging netting. However, I'm saving my bitterest obscenities for my agent, who thought this was a great idea in the first place.

The sergeant is still hurling abuse way above me as I finally scramble to my knees and stagger to the net ladder. The rope is coarse, scrubbing against my mud-encrusted hands as I crawl wearily up it, towards the wooden pole at the top. I tumble over it and begin my descent, half-falling, half-clawing my way back down.

Then it is the real killer, the one I've been dreading. The monkey bars.

Hot bath, hot bath, I chant to myself as I watch the others before me swing competently over the waiting stream. It's obviously a boy thing, like spin-bowling or ball control with the feet. Up ahead, a soldier falls and is greeted with more verbal abuse. He plods back past me to have another go, unable to resist flashing his eyes up and down my camouflage-covered body.

Halfway across, and my arms feel like jelly. The soldier is already behind me, telling me to get a bloody move on. It ruins my concentration and I land in the sand. My legs buckle, sending me almost face down in it. I come up blinking and spluttering, wiping the sand out of my eyes. I must look a sight, I think sourly, with soaking wet hair dulling its usual lustrous sheen, and spattered with earth from bedraggled head to combat boots. Cursing my previous assumption that the whole military training thing would be fun, I trudge onwards. A splash up ahead warns me of what is to come.

More mud, and a yawning ditch, over which dangles a soggy rope. My nemesis. The boys are waiting on the other side, shouting encouragement. I know I'm definitely going to get wet this time. Wetter, even. The knotty rope is thrust into my weakened fingers. It is high, and too short to allow me to have a proper run at it.

I'm suspended four feet above the water – the bank with the boys on it a distant dream, the bank with the sergeant on it a waiting nightmare. There is no way out of my predicament except down. For a moment I wriggle like a caught fish, before realising the futility of my pathetic struggling. I can feel the top half of my uniform separating from the bottom half, baring my stomach to twenty pairs of hungry eyes. If I go down now, they'll have even more to stare at. Belatedly, I think maybe a *balconette* bra isn't the most sensible thing to wear on an assault course.

My fingers are slipping, and I know I'm not going to make it. I hang there by my fingertips, fighting the inevitable, while the others shout, 'In, in, in!' Lovely boys, bless them ...

The water is a cold shock, making me gasp. I scramble up the bank straight away, weighed down by the sodden fatigues and heavy boots. This time I will make it. It is a matter of pride. I take a run at the rope, and for one horrible second think I am going to miss it and take another muddy dive into the ditch. But no, it is in my hands, and I am swinging towards the bank, the boys reaching for me with outstretched hands. I land in their arms, exultant, energised enough to whoop with triumph. The boys stand silently, gawping like teenagers, transfixed by my soaking wet T-shirt. The white material clings to my body, clearly outlining my breasts and nipples, made firm by the coldness of the water. I stand with hands on hips, staring back at them defiantly. Though I don't actually mind them looking. It has probably been a long time since they've seen a real flesh-and-blood woman who isn't trussed up in the same uniform they're wearing.

'All right, you lot. What is this, a slumber party? Get back to barracks and clean off!' The sergeant has walked over a bridge near where the rope is still swaying gently.

The spell is broken. We scramble into line and march back to the garrison.

All handsome, strong young men, they have been very sweet to me since my arrival that morning. I've been sent there for a magazine feature on being a trainee soldier and so far, after being plastered with mud and dragged through endless drill practice, I'm glad I didn't choose the Army as a career.

'In the shower, you lot. Girls go first. Titmuss, I know you qualify as being a girl but on this occasion you'll be with the boys. Move!'

It feels weird, disrobing in the shower with the men just behind a small wall, waiting for me to finish, but there is no time for anxieties about privacy. I strip off really quickly and dart under the water. The fragrance of fruity shampoo soon fills the steamy air. I stand under the hot needles of water, luxuriating in the relief of being clean as they cascade over my body, warming it through. The miserable autumn weather has not let up, I have been soaked to the skin more than once since barely passing military muster this morning, and am now chilled to the bone. A dirty pool of water and suds gathers at my feet. The boys are waiting beyond the glossy white brick wall, smelling my girly aroma and longing for a glimpse as I run the soap all over my body. In my mind they actually are watching, and I am putting on a show, my hands running over my body, massaging the suds in, the lather flowing over my hands like cream. I can imagine them all, lost in their own dirty thoughts, hard and in rapture at this blonde goddess among them, lifting her breasts as though offering them as gifts.

And how would I seduce Sergeant Woods, with his deep Scottish voice and fierce blue eyes? He would scrub up pretty well in a kilt, I think. All firm thighs and muscled shoulders, broad of chest and powerful enough to stop a girl struggling. When he was making me do press-ups in front of the troops earlier that day, and bawling me out for not polishing my shoes to a high enough shine, I had been thinking what I would give to have him under my control. The threat of a bit of extreme drill hanging over him? I like it. What would he do then, faced with being under the orders of a blonde taskmistress?

'Times up,' he barks, cutting short my reverie. I drop the shower gel bottle. It slithers across the floor towards his feet. As I grope for it he is watching my naked butt, glaring at me like an angry eagle. 'This isn't a health club, missy. Get your kit back on.' He throws me a towel. 'Uniform inspection in fifteen minutes,' he says.

Has he been watching me all along? I detect a certain hoarseness in his voice. Thinking about the implications of that I take the towel and walk out, just as the boys are filing in. They all wear expressions of wanting to look, but not daring to.

That night, after chowing down a surprisingly good beef stew, and making a few notes on my laptop, I crash out on my bed. A thin mattress and lumpy pillow have never felt so luxurious. The thick woollen blanket feels like cashmere, but I'm not sure the squaddies have such treats. I'm so tired, I don't move until I'm rudely woken up at six the following morning.

The regiment is on the move. We're going on night manoeuvres somewhere in the middle of Wales. Great, I think. More rain. It has stopped for now, though leaden clouds seem to be just waiting for us to set up camp later on that afternoon.

Glen gives me a hand up into a camouflaged Defender, and we haul out in convoy. It is like being transported in a cattle truck, although my fellow travellers are a lot more appealing. Freshly showered and shaved, with short-cropped hair and solid, muscular bodies, these men are in top physical condition and are enjoying having someone smaller and less robust to look after.

'Have you put up a tent before?' Gaz asks me, in a deep, mellifluous voice. He is black-skinned and glossy, with a dazzling white smile.

'I haven't *slept* in a tent before,' I reply. I'm a little apprehensive, being stuck in the middle of a wild landscape, with nothing but a few feet of canvas to protect me from the elements.

'Don't worry, we'll look out for you,' Rik assures me with a grin. He explains what's happening. We will be setting up camp halfway up a Welsh mountainside, and one of the men will lose himself in the forest, attempting to reach a hut on the other side of the mountain; the others must track him down before sunset. I have a choice. To be the hunter, or the hunted. I like the idea of being hunted by a group of strapping men, so I volunteer to be with the prey.

'You'd better be able to keep quiet,' Gaz says, with another dazzling smile and a wink. He seems to relish the challenge of being saddled with a blonde who is more comfortable getting lost in the West End. I respond to his easy smile with one of my own. An anticipatory tingle creeps down my spine.

The Land Rover bounces us down the dual carriageway, draughty and creaky and uncomfortable. I cannot see the scenery changing, so when we eventually unfold ourselves from the back, the mountains surrounding us are a shock. The clouds have been ripped to shreds by a keen wind, leaving a soft blue sky behind them. Below us, the forest, tall pines on the tree line, and below that, deciduous, older oak and beech, glowing golden in the gentle autumn sun. The men are already pulling equipment out of the convoy of Defenders, shrugging on huge rucksacks, and consulting maps and compasses. The camp site is two miles into the wilderness, and we will be walking it. My rucksack is slightly smaller, bearing my tent, sleeping bag, a billycan, spare clothes, and a notebook.

The boys are cheerful as we set off along the path. There is a gate, covered with barbed wire to keep the public out, and a sign saying MILITARY TRAINING ZONE – DO NOT CROSS in large enough letters to keep the most militant rambler at bay. Then we veer off the path and head down towards the tree line. It isn't long before we are in deep forest, moving slower this time. My rucksack occasionally gets caught on a low branch, but there is always someone on hand to help me out. They are attentive, making sure I can keep up, that I'm not getting tired.

'You're doing all right,' Rik says to me with a grin, and I'm grateful to him. I don't want to be a burden on these men. I feel strong and capable as we stride along, the leaves crunching under our feet. It hasn't rained here as much as it has in Wiltshire, and there is very little mud.

We set up camp in a small, mossy clearing in the woods. I struggle with my smaller tent, watching how the others are competently putting up theirs. The aluminium poles seem to thwart me every time. The sergeant watches me, shaking his head in dismay, before ordering one of the other men to give me a lesson how to do it properly. There is much amusement as I wrestle with one of the poles. As I get one end into the ground, the other springs out, as I haven't hammered it in far enough. They're amused by some colourful language before the wretched thing is up, and with a groundsheet in place and a thick, downy sleeping bag, it looks quite cosy. Very cosy, in fact. I would have to be very good friends with someone to let them share it. The inside looks barely large enough to fit me, never mind anyone else.

I don't have time to contemplate how it is going to feel sleeping inside it, though. As soon as the camp is set up we are receiving our orders. As the hunted, Gaz and I have to set off first, and as he intends to put as much distance as possible between us and the rest of the garrison, we have to move fast.

We walk for a mile, skimming the line of trees before moving off into open, scrubby mountain country. Gaz consults his map.

'We want to get to that forest there. Once we are under cover of the trees, they'll have one hell of a job finding us. But first ...' He looks up the mountain and grins at me.

'Don't tell me.' I start walking up the mountain. He stops me.

'Not yet. They could still spot us. We need to move further round.'

So we do, and then we start to trail up over the scrubby terrain. When my legs start letting me down his strong, dark hand is there to pull me along. Before long, we are dropping back down, but not before I take in the view. The mountains are like a vast, rumpled, purple-tinged blanket, studded with tiny white sheep, dark clumps of trees and a slow river sinuously carving its way through the valley below. The forest we are intending to lose ourselves in is a mixed tangle of oak and ash and beech, with a large grey lake at its leading edge.

By the time we reach it the light is fading, and with it, there is an insidious drop in temperature. The forest is dark and dense, but his hand is comforting as he leads me through the undergrowth.

'They might have figured we would head for here,' he says in a whisper, hunkering down to the ground. We consult the map again, and he taps the spot we need to aim for. I like the way he listens to my suggestions instead of treating me like a helpless passenger. We decide that heading straight for the lake would be too dangerous. There is too much risk of getting spotted from the other side. 'The trees will be thinner there. We need to keep at least a hundred yards back in,' he explains when I ask why.

'Are their guns loaded?' I ask, out of interest.

He smiles again, showing very white teeth in his camouflaged face. 'You scared?'

'Excited,' I reply, sparkling at him. Now that night is near, there is an extra element of danger that has not been present before. Every footstep, every inadvertently snapped twig, could give us away. A heavy dew is falling on the ground, permeating the air with the earthy smell of rotting leaves. The mountains are losing their colour, merging into one ominous mass.

Gaz squeezes my hand suddenly and motions to me to be silent. We crouch down. I'm trying to control my breathing. Adrenaline, awakened by his touch, has made it quicken. Just in time we see another shadowy figure, clutching a rifle in readiness, creeping along just yards in front of us. The hut is about a quarter of a mile ahead, but this place is teeming with highly trained men and their sole focus is to find us. I begin to wonder whether we will make it. There is a shuffling sound very close by us, tiny and indistinct. I press closer to Gaz, and feel him move against me, a hard, muscular arm around my waist. Subtly it creeps up under my jacket to feel my breast.

'It's a wood mouse,' he breathes, motioning to the direction of the noise. In the fast fading light I can see its pink tail, disappearing under a pile of leaves. I don't withdraw from Gaz, though. The warmth of his hand feels lovely seeping through my T-shirt, into my breast. He captures the nipple between two fingers, tugging it gently. 'Keep very quiet,' he breathes in my ear. His manly scent is as musky and earthen as the forest.

In reply I press my lips against his cheek, and sense, rather than hear, him catch his breath.

There is a sneeze, to my right. It could have been another innocent woodland creature, but Gaz doesn't think so. It's time for the night goggles. Putting them on, we advance forward, cautiously, following the first figure we had seen. Gaz looks alien in his, and I feel strange in mine. The whole woodland has come alive with black-and-grey movement. Trees rustling, the eyes of animals glinting and disappearing, the undergrowth shifting beyond our feet with insects and small mammals. By now it is almost completely dark, and the hut is a dark hump against the mountainous skyline.

We reach it unmolested, and grab the flag we have been assigned to rescue. I am shaking with triumph, but Gaz warns me it isn't over yet.

'We need to get back to base before we get spotted,' he reminds me. At that moment we spot two figures running in a crouch towards the hut from the other side. We are in serious danger of being caught. Gaz hisses at me to follow and we dive for the woods, this time not caring about the leaves crunching accusingly under our feet. Deep in the dark I trip, and we land together on the soft ground. Gaz holds me close, listening for signs that we might have been detected. I can smell his earthy deodorant, working overtime, and the faint undertones of loamy leaves and hot male. He is as aware of me, his face buried in my neck to stifle his heavy breathing. It is only natural for our lips to meet in a hungry, adrenaline-fuelled kiss, our bodies pushing urgently against each other. In the middle distance, a small group of lean, alert men, all with their weapons at the ready, are scanning the woods for any sign that we might be there. Gaz remembers this, struggling to concentrate on the task in hand like a drowning man fighting to reach the water's surface.

'We'll head north,' he says in a ragged whisper, rising to his feet. As he does, there is a metallic click, and a dark voice barking, 'Freeze!'

The woodland becomes alive. Camouflaged, grinning men appear from every direction, emerging from behind bushes and trees. Where had they come from?

We are taken from our hiding place back to the lake, and marched back to the camp.

The atmosphere back at the cluster of tents is of a job well done. I scribble some notes and inhale the glorious smell of cooking sausages. Not exactly a model's ideal supper, but what the hell! I'm not about to demand a GI-friendly bean salad and fresh fruit dessert. A mug of strong hot tea is thrust into my cold hands. Gradually, the heat from the fire warms my aching feet and stiff joints. Sausages, onions and beans have never tasted so good.

In the soft firelight, the men talk and laugh, recounting stories of past manoeuvres. They ask me questions about my life in London, and how I am finding being out here with them and having no agents or media types to protect me.

'But I have you to protect me,' I say. 'I feel very safe.'

'That's brave of you,' someone says. It's Rik, the big blond bear. He mentions he's seen my picture in a magazine recently. As I was naked at the time, I blush, but fortunately no one can see.

'Glad you liked it,' I say, and a thought comes to me. I would be leaving the next day and they had been so good to me. It is time I gave something back. 'You want to see them for real?'

They agree that would be very nice. Actually, I'm surprised their roar of approval isn't heard in London. It's a lovely feeling, stripping off in the flattering glow of the fire, with the primeval faces of fit, hungry men watching. I take the jacket off first, letting them see my white T-shirt. The cool night air has made my nipples as hard as bullets, and stretching the material over them only enhances that loaded-weapon effect. They sigh with approval as I peel the T-shirt away, revealing a gauzy white bra. The material is translucent, showing the shadows surrounding my nipples. Gaz licks his lips, remembering those few snatched moments in the deep woodland. Warmth from the fire licks at my skin, keeping me comfortable as I push down the khaki combat trousers over and off the boots and stand in my small white matching thong panties. Wadding my trousers into a cushion, I sit on them and smile at the boys.

'Anyone care to pass me another sausage?'

They get a real kick out of having me among them, clad only in my underwear and sturdy boots. I'm excited by it as well, sensing their desire, knowing they cannot do anything about it but dying to have a go, see how far they can push it. Even the dour Scottish sergeant makes a few lusty jokes.

Eventually it's time for bed, though I doubt if many of them will get to sleep very easily. I don't, because the night is yielding sounds I have never heard before. Tiny rustlings, soft grunts, the whoosh of breath from one of the other tents, I hope. An owl decides to sit above us, and starts calling for its mate in a voice ringing throughout the forest. Eventually the sergeant shouts at it and it flies away, but it can still be heard, singing its mournful song.

For a while I lie listening to it, breathing in the sexy earth smells of mulch and grass and pine needles. And, very softly, my name being called.

It happens again and I unzip my tent, poking my head out to see who is speaking. Gaz is sitting in the entrance of his small tent, looking pensive in the waning firelight, beckoning to me. The thought of lying with him in a warm sleeping bag is full of promise, so I creep over to where he is, but before I can crawl into the tent Sergeant Woods has spotted me. We exchange a few words and I hurry back to my tent without disturbing anyone else. On my mind is the punishment he will mete out to me tomorrow.

The journey back to the barracks is long and uncomfortable. We are all in desperate need of a wash and some fresh clothes after the three-hour journey. I exchange a look with the sergeant as we march back to the barrack-room showers.

'Keep your kit on,' he orders me, to the surprise of the boys.

I go in and obediently stand under the spray of the middle shower, fully dressed. My clothes are tight and uncomfortable, clinging to my body in all the right places. The boys come in and line up against the opposite wall, looking a little uncertain. The sergeant joins them.

'Get your kit off,' he says to them. 'Keep your underpants on. If you've gone commando today, that's bad luck. When you've done, fold your arms across your chests.'

I see what he is intending to do. Will this be the pinnacle of my punishment? It seems more like the pinnacle of theirs. Soon they are standing in their trunks, toned and muscular and gorgeous.

'This exercise is about discipline, which last night you so obviously lacked,' Woods says, walking up and down in front of them, the baton under his arm. 'Do you have the discipline not to rise to the temptation she presents?' He grins evilly. 'We're going to find out.'

I can see that Gaz has failed already, and I'm not even undressed yet. He looks smug, proud of his prodigious gifts. The others have nothing to be ashamed of either. Tight white trunks, small tangas, all filled to bursting.

Sergeant Woods approaches me. 'Now you can strip,' he says.

There is a certain danger in being the only woman in a room full of half-naked, red-blooded men, all muscles and balls, and being told to take my clothes off in front of them only adds to the nervous excitement I'm feeling.

Firstly I remove my boots and ease the mud-smeared khaki combats over my hips, revealing tiny white panties that quickly turn translucent under the relentless shower spray. Standing in small white ankle socks, the panties and my wet T-shirt, I wink at the boys. A couple of them shift from foot to foot, embarrassed at the reaction I am provoking in them. Making eye contact with Gaz and holding it, I slowly pull the material of my T-shirt away from my breasts and let it go, letting it ping back and grab them ever more intimately. The reaction is instantaneous. As one by one they succumb to nature's calling, the sergeant watches approvingly, obviously enjoying himself. I squeeze some shower gel into my palm and then run it through my hair, ridding myself of the horrid mud and surrounding myself in floral steam. Turning slowly around, easing my panties up over my cheeks and staring back at them, I bite my lower lip. I know the moves. Know how to untie their knots of frustration and longing. They are staring, unashamed now of their excitement.

I turn again to face them, running my hands down my thighs, letting my breasts swing forward.

Sergeant Woods glances at his men, all standing with their arms folded across their chests, sporting a squad of fine erections, and he looks almost proud of them.

'Go get her, boys,' he says.

The squaddies don't need any more encouragement. One by one they strip off their underpants. Their finely toned bodies gleam in the harsh overhead lighting. Someone turns the other showers on. The room fills with steam. Sergeant Woods stands at ease, hands clasped behind his back, and watches events unfold as I am surrounded by beautiful, muscular young men of every hue, from cream to dusky brown to darkest black, all eager to wash me down, to run their hands over my body, and to relieve the ache caused by an existence in single-sex barracks. I lean back against one brawny chest and revel in the crowd of hands. I don't know how many, but I am smothered. Wet T-shirt whipped off, bra snapped away, socks pinched off my toes, I am unwrapped for the squaddies' mess. Eager paws weigh and squeeze my breasts, stroke buttocks and stomach, and when I feel the first flicker of a tongue against a nipple I let out a sigh and arch my back to invite more. But no one needs any encouragement in the steam room. Hands and tongues go everywhere, and my own palms are quickly filled with rigid male muscle. Under the beating water I am stroked and invaded and toyed with, barely able to stand as the steamy heat and overwhelming arousal weakens my body. Gaz lifts me, and sets me down on the massive girth I was admiring earlier. I don't have to make any effort as those big strong boys do it for me, holding me under the arms and moving me with military precision up and down his slick tool. Espresso black velvet against cream silk, I hardly have time to enjoy our erotic entwining as another anonymous man clasps me from behind, and rubs itself against me. My world has been reduced to slippery skin, hard flesh, swarming hands, hungry mouths. I surrender to all of it, allow them to take complete control and reduce me to a plaything. Soon I am doused with more than just water. Warm and thick, they splash themselves over my willing body, before their offerings are quickly washed down the drains. I bend down to pleasure the mighty Gaz and immediately feel Rik slide inside me, up to the hilt. He takes my hair and twists it in his fingers, riding me like a wild horse. Gaz is pressed flat against the wet wall, unable to move as he enjoys the consequences of Rik's desperate thrusting.

And throughout, the stone-faced sergeant watches, his cold face showing no emotion, even when I am the one against the wall, with Glen, one of the quieter ones, skilfully seeking out my swollen bud. He is very good, and I keep eye contact with the sergeant as I am transported to ecstasy for a few sweet seconds, my hot little cries of pleasure ringing around the tiled room. My vision fades, but still I keep him in my sight, panting as Glen finishes me off with a long, slow shag against the wall, groaning loudly in my ear as he screws himself dry.

Afterwards, when I'm dressed and respectable, Sergeant Woods comes to say farewell. He is smiling for the first time as he shakes my hand, very formally and stiffly.

'You would make a lousy soldier,' he says, a twinkle in his eyes, 'but you're great for morale, lass.'

10

Audience of One

I am sitting in the glamorous Art Deco surroundings of Claridges in Mayfair, London, staring absently into my cocktail glass, trying not to recall the events of an evening that started so well and ended about 45 minutes later. I focus on the melting lozenge of ice in my Manhattan, pondering on the usual subject of why it's so difficult to find someone who is genuinely interested in me and not just chasing the glamour. Idle flirtation at various parties and the eventual gravitational pull of mutual attraction had resulted in my date asking me for dinner, and my insouciant agreement. The stereotypical tall, handsome, dark and rich achiever, he so obviously fancied me I was surprised that his heart wasn't visibly pounding by the time the casual reply tripped from my dry lips.

Now I'm sitting in this beautiful bar, not half a mile from the restaurant I had walked out of, in my exorbitantly expensive Little Black Dress and Jimmy Choos, and the most galling thing I can think of is that I thought he was worth the Choos in the first place. For a start, his gaze didn't travel any further down than my chest, and I doubt whether it noticed the carefully chosen, exquisitely delicate diamond choker, with matching earrings, either. I looked a million dollars, and the arsehole didn't even comment. He thought I was too dumb to notice that he was more interested in the contents of my bra than my head. We didn't even get past the entrées.

Hope he's enjoying his braised duck. It's the only dish he'll conquer tonight, I think grimly, stabbing at a green olive. I stopped by Claridges to console myself with a cocktail, to indulge in a little luxury before I go home to a deep bath to lick my wounds.

The bar isn't busy. At the other end of the counter a man sits, looking pensive, nursing a whisky tumbler. He's wearing a beautiful suit in an unusual dark-purple. He looks vaguely familiar. I can't see him properly and I don't want to stare. Yet I am intrigued. Every so often he lifts the glass to his lips, not looking left or right. There is a sense of poignancy around him, of private angst more acute than my own. I look away, but not before he glances towards me and sees me watching him. We are like two figures in an Edward Hopper painting. Not exactly nighthawks, but the atmosphere's the same.

I don't want him to think I'm trying to catch his eye. The last thing I want is to be chatted up by yet another bloke who thinks he's in with a chance for a quickie with an attractive unaccompanied young woman.

He's watching me, though. Maybe he thinks he's recognised me. I stab another olive, but the cocktail stick misses and the damned thing goes skidding across the bar. The bartender rescues it with a wintry smile and wipes the residue away. I give up on the olives and bury my nose in my drink. Unable to resist, I look the man's way again. He is smiling. Not laughing, or grinning, just smiling, in a quirky, half-reluctant way that warns me he isn't trying to flirt. It is who I thought it was. Oh my God. I hope my lips mirror the same sentiment, although I am now beginning to wish he would approach me. We could share our sorrows, kiss each other on the cheek at the end of it and just go our separate ways.

Companionship. Yes, that's it. That's what I want and need ...

I sense movement beside me. Here we go, I think, another arsehole. At least in Claridges one meets a better class of arsehole; probably less likely to take offence when I blow them out. I look up, ready with my polite no-thank-yous.

It's him. I'm surprised, because I didn't think he looked in the mood. And I'm shocked, because it dawns on me just how famous this guy is and here I am about to have a private audience.

I need a distraction; something to do with my hands to disguise my sudden sense of panic. An olive. I stab at a glossy black one and put it in my mouth. It's very bitter. I grimace, and he laughs this time.

'Why do you eat them if you don't like them?' is his opening gambit.

'They're like some men. They look good until you taste them.' I dab at my lips with a tiny napkin and avoid his eyes. He looks genuinely amused.

'That applies to women as well,' he says.

'Some women,' I correct him.

He nodded. 'Somebody must have pissed you off tonight.'

'How did you guess?' My tongue feels as if it has swollen to twice its size. He's taller than the media would have everyone believe, and almost impossibly suave in that eye-catching suit, as if he's just left the set of a fashion shoot. Those eyes, dark as melted chocolate, are looking deep into my soul. And the eyelashes are thick and long. He knows how to use them, how to turn women on. That, as well as the seductive songs he sings, is the key to his success. I have watched him in the past on television, mesmerised, wanting to know, like millions of other women, what he would be like in bed. And he's right here, in Claridges, talking to me about ... what? I realise I haven't been listening. I try to focus, pulling my mind back to sensible conversation, which I bet he doesn't hear a whole lot of, moving in the world of big league music producers and A&R men.

'A woman dresses like you and sits alone in a bar for two reasons,' he's saying. 'She's had a row with her date, or she wants to get laid.'

'A man dresses like you on his own for one reason. He's been stood up,' I counter.

'I guess I deserved that.'

'Better than a slap in the face. It looks like it's the last thing you need right now. I walked out on my date, by the way. He was being a prick.'

'Why?'

I am taken aback. Why would he want to know, anyway? He's concentrating on my face and not once seems tempted to glance lower down. Maybe he's just very, very good at seduction.

'He was too busy watching my boobs to have a decent conversation,' I say, challenging him to drop his gaze. It doesn't waver once. This man was good. Or he really wasn't interested. Hopefully the former.

'Good for you,' he says, and points to my glass. 'Another cocktail?'

I point to his. 'Another whisky? You look as if you need it more than I do.'

An almost indiscernible hesitation, as if trying to assess the game I'm playing, before he nods to the bartender. He gets busy.

'No games,' I say, hoping I've read him correctly.

He relaxes slightly, and sticks out his hand for me to shake, telling me his name.

I take his hand, hoping mine doesn't feel too clammy, and introduce myself.

'I know,' he says, with a winning smile.

'Relax, I'm not after your body,' I say pertly, giving him a dazzling smile.

'I could take that as an insult.' He picks up his replenished drink and swirls the amber liquid nonchalantly around the bottom, obviously enjoying the role of sophisticated lounge lizard.

'It's more of an assumption, by some men.'

'Oh yes, those men again.' He watches as I sip my drink. I'm not being coy, or openly flirtatious, and it obviously intrigues him. I'm not what he has previously assumed I would be like, just as he isn't the wild find 'em, fuck 'em, forget 'em rock god I had been expecting. 'Those men and those women should just find each other and shag themselves stupid, shouldn't they?'

'And leave us in peace,' I agree.

'It would be a shame to waste this opportunity, though,' he says, with a wicked grin.

'You are your own worst enemy.' I wag my finger admonishingly at him. 'You moan about not being able to find the right woman but you won't find her while you're hanging around with star-fuckers, present company excepted, of course.'

'What about you? You're exhibiting yourself at every opportunity!'

'That's business. Nothing to do with who I am inside. Anyway, that's irrelevant. If a girl has a great body *some men* will always look at the obvious bits first. It's human nature.'

'So what are you worried about? This poor guy gets you to dinner, and you blow him out because he's looking at your tits?'

'You don't know the whole story.' I sound defensive, and hate it. 'I want a guy to take me to dinner because he sees something more than just big tits and a nice smile.'

'Sorry,' he says suddenly. 'I didn't mean to offend you.'

That cost him a lot, I can tell.

'Hey, it's OK.' I resist the temptation to cover his hand with my own. 'So what's your trouble? Why's a popular boy like you sitting in a bar on his own?'

He stares thoughtfully into his drink. 'Because I'm knackered. Been filming since just after dawn, doing take after take. I just sometimes like to be somewhere discreet and anonymous, like this, to unwind, where I know I'm not going to be hounded. And I didn't feel like heading home just yet.'

There is a companionable silence between us as we drink and look around the bar. People are coming out of the dining room, having enjoyed a superlative meal at Ramsay's restaurant, and are slowly making their way up the staircase. A few come to the bar, buy their nightcaps and sit in plush sofas to finish off conversations before going to bed. Some glance our way, but they are either too posh or too uninterested to care who we are and what we are doing. We continue talking as the hands on the clock shift towards midnight. I'm not sure if I buy his explanation about being tired. He looks to me as if he's hurting about some recent betrayal and needs to talk, so I listen, sympathetic because of what has happened to me in the past.

His dark eyes penetrate mine. 'I guess I just want someone I can trust, who can hold me at the end of the day and just tell me I'm doing OK.' He looks ruefully at his glass. 'Shit, I think I've had too many of these. You know how it feels,' he says. 'Half the guys back in my hotel suite talk bullshit. I'm their meal ticket, but if I piss one of them off, I'm gossip fodder in the magazines.' His finger moves and begins to caress mine. 'I'd love to see the headlines tomorrow if anyone saw us two.'

'My stock would go up overnight,' I say jokingly, moving my hand away. I don't want him thinking that is the reason I am attempting to seduce him.

But hold on ... that wasn't my intention. I'm merely talking to him as a friend. If he makes a move, how friendly will I be then?

'You're a clever girl,' he says, draining his glass. 'For all I know, you've been tipped the nod that I would be here tonight.'

'I could, but it's not the case. Though you could also go to the tabloids and say I was the most fantastic woman you'd ever had. I wouldn't mind.' I grin at him mischievously. He lifts one dark eyebrow in a mock-sardonic gesture and leans closer to me.

'I'm not going to talk about something I don't know to be true.'

We exchange a conspiratorial look. I am not bold enough to say, 'Why don't you find out?' But the words linger between us. When did this conversation become so suggestive? I'm not sure I know or care, and neither does he. He picks up the cocktail stick, spearing the cherry in my glass, and slides it off, holding it to my lips. I let him feed me, and his fingers linger over my bottom lip for a second before he licks the moisture away from their tips.

'I say forget the press. Bloody jackals.' He slides off the seat. 'I'll be back in a minute.'

One part of me doubts he will be, but it isn't long before he is by my side again.

'Let's go,' he murmurs in my ear. I don't ask where, and he doesn't say.

We share the lift with a woman in a cashmere wrap and her gentleman friend in a black dinner jacket. I like a man in a tuxedo. It gives him a certain clout. I feel a cold finger of anticipation travel up my spine as I look at his reflection, broad-shouldered in the tailored black jacket. The door opens and the couple walk out with murmured, very English, goodnights. We carry on up and up, to the top floor.

'You're a bad boy,' I whisper.

'That's what a bad girl needs,' he replies.

My stilettos sink into the luxuriously thick carpet in the corridor. The smell of lilies permeates the air from an elaborate arrangement on a side table in a large alcove. There is a large mirror, but I dare not look into it, as if seeing my reflection would break the spell I am under.

He stops by a door, and pauses theatrically. 'Ready?'

Before I can reply he has opened the door into the room.

But not just one room. A suite. A sumptuous suite dominated by a grand piano next to a tall window, the city lights sparkling softly outside. The drawing-room area consists of comfortable couches in vibrant colours, with overstuffed cushions, and exotic swags and tails surrounding the windows.

The champagne is by the canopied bed, ready-chilled. Soft music plays in the background. There are impressive flower arrangements using those lovely tropical orange pointy flowers on sticks with velvety buds. A backdrop of silk gleams in the soft light.

'You like it?' he asks. It's as if he wants approval, which is strange for a man worth millions.

'It's beautiful,' I say, and he smiles, almost shyly.

'I thought we deserved the best. Just a bedroom seemed ...' he gropes for the word.

'Presumptuous?' I offer.

'Something like that. Champagne?' he asks, but I shake my head.

'Not yet.' I run a hand through my hair and trace my right index finger from his collarbone down to the waistband of his trousers. He shivers in response.

He's wearing a silk tie that's loosened but now it's coming off completely. He lets me tug it free. It slips from under his collar with a sibilant hiss. He picks up the cue and guides me back against the door, covering my lips with his. His kiss is urgent, flavoured with single malt, but I hardly have time to register the taste before our tongues entwine, slippery and eager. His breath is hot on my cheek. I can feel an even more urgent thrusting lower down, much lower, but though my hands itch to caress it I save that pleasure for later. I cannot believe this pop music icon is pressing his cock against me; that we are this close to doing something that would have the press wild for details. But they're not going to know.

I push his jacket from his shoulders as he devours my neck, slightly scuffing my skin with the beginnings of dark bristles. It falls to the ground in a dark, crumpled pool of cashmere. I can smell my perfume, my body heat, mingling with his spicy aftershave. His hair is short and spiky, yet soft to the touch as I comb my fingers through it, waiting for this first heated moment of passion to pass. Finally he looks down at me, slightly dishevelled; he is breathing as heavily as I am.

'You're gorgeous,' he whispers, hungrily kissing me again.

'Thank you,' I whisper back, caressing his face. He is so full of need, so vulnerable, that my heart swells and my body lifts naturally towards his. I slip my fingers into the waistband of his trousers and pull him towards me for another kiss.

'The doorway is great, but I presume you've paid for the rest of the suite as well?'

Another quirky smile twists those divine lips. He takes my hand and leads me into the room. I catch a glimpse of our reflections in a large dressing-table mirror near the bed. The light is flattering, suffusing our skin with warm, honey tones. I am glad I wore my coral and gold bra and the tiny thong that went with it. My date would probably have been lucky tonight, had he not been such an arse. His loss.

I'm smiling as I watch the fingers in the mirror slowly gathering up the hem of my dress. He turns me around so that he too can benefit from the view, and a sudden jolt in his lower regions tells me he approves. He digs his fingers into my peachy backside and growls softly in his throat. I move so I can see his face.

'You're a bottom man?'

'And a tit man, and a legs man.' He lets the dress fall again, his eyes on mine. 'But that isn't why we're here.'

I slowly shake my head in agreement. He picks up my hand and kisses it in an oddly courtly gesture. The tip of his tongue comes out and traces around the top of my middle finger. The delicate touch sends shivers right through my body. He licks each finger in turn, all the while unbuttoning his shirt, and the twin gestures cause a rippling wave of desire right through me. It doesn't stop as he sets the hand free before pressing gentle kisses over my face, my throat, my neck. Every one of them feels like the kiss of a dove's wing. I had no idea that a man who seemed to thrive on entertaining thousands of people at once could be so accomplished, yet here he is doing things to my body and my senses which are so far removed from the usual lures of money, fame and power.

As he moves down, slipping my dress off one shoulder, my breath becomes unsteady. My nipples are hard and yearning, just waiting for the hot moisture of his lips. I am biting my lip, arching towards him, unable to stop myself, but before he reaches the holy grail of my breasts he moves me back towards the bed and lays me upon it. I wriggle upwards and begin to unzip my dress, but he stops me.

'What's the hurry? We'll be here all night.'

A pleasurable tingle shoots through my body. This is no ordinary one-night stand. Something is happening between us. Something cerebral, uniting us in a way most people only dream of. In a moment I am in his arms and being kissed among mountainous goose-down pillows. He is enjoying just kissing me, building our anticipation. As his hand almost shyly feels for my breast I understand what he needs. It is as if he wants to be a teenager again, tentatively questing for pleasure, but with the experience of a fully grown man when it really matters. My hand covers his, encouraging him, letting him feel the weight of my breast through the black silk dress before guiding his hand down to the hem. I feel his fingers against the silk of my stockings, transferring his heat to my flesh. His shirt comes away from the waistband and my hands are waiting, cool and soft, to stroke the pale skin underneath. His body is familiar from the videos I've seen, and the hair is dark and silky on his chest. Playfully I tweak his nipple, which hardens like a little seed. Pushing him on his back, I flip his shirt open and flick the nipple with my tongue. Then the other, until it too is hard and tingling. As he moans with surprised pleasure I sit on him, pinning him to the bed. He fits very nicely between my legs, pulsing promisingly as I unfasten his shirt and flip it open.

'Very nice,' I purr, running my hands all over his body.

'Can I do the same to you?' he asks.

I unzip my dress at the back and pull it over my head, tossing it carelessly away. I'm revealed in my shapely glory, hands on hips, breasts reaching out to him. He's seen it all before, no doubt, in various glossy male magazines, but nothing is ever as good as the real thing, and this shows in his face as he reaches to outline my curves with trembling hands, his body underneath mine rising in an attempt to claim me for his own.

'Leave it on,' he says, as I reach around to unfasten my pretty bra. 'It's beautiful.' He sits up and shrugs off his shirt, pulling me back onto him. The warmth of our bodies makes us both smile before he kisses me again, this time flipping me onto my back. Slowly he presses kisses, hot and light, all over my body, until it feels as if I am being showered with rose petals. He is moving downwards; I hold my breath, tensing as his breath brushes against my thighs, letting loose a little whimper as he hovers over my centre, then moves on down again, his fingers toying with the flesh above my stocking tops. My stockings are so fine I can feel every feathering of lips against skin as he moves down to my feet to admire my beautiful and delicate Jimmy Choos. Suddenly, the money spent seems a bargain, as he gives them due respect before unfastening the tiny buckle at my ankle. As the shoe comes away he kisses the sole of my foot, then my big toe, causing a jolt of sensation so fierce I have to draw away.

With implicit understanding he leaves it alone and moves to the other foot, removing the shoe, placing them both gently next to the bed as if he realises how expensive and fragile they are. Then more kisses, up my other leg, his tongue swirling around the tops of my thighs. I am so aroused by this time it is tempting just to scream at him to do me right then, but I know what he's doing. He's drawing out the moment, as a fine pianist does with a magnificent concerto. A sly tongue, flicking around my expectant centre, sets me quivering. The pillows take full punishment from my clenched hands as he hovers there, tasting, eliciting tiny moans from my parted lips. Wantonly I spread myself wider, knowing that he would move away, making me wait, but he doesn't. He's settling down, savouring my woman flavour as a gourmet relishes a banquet. He's good, so good I can hardly concentrate on who it is doing this to me, just the feeling of soaring, swelling, bursting with sensation as the orgasm hits and he stays there, keeping it going, his hands tight on my buttocks to stop me squirming away. In the end it is too much and I twist from him, panting, wild, wanting him to thrust inside me right then.

He holds me for a moment, stroking my leg, gentling me, before reaching for my suspenders. I sit up, saying I will do it, taking a moment to recover from the body-shattering orgasm I have just enjoyed.

He sits back among the pillows as I open the champagne, secretly admiring my reflection as I handle the bottle and cork. Damned sexy, if I do say so myself. The cork comes free with a soft pop and I pour the precious liquid into two crystal flutes, handing one to him.

'As you say, what's the hurry?'

He lifts his glass, and sits back to enjoy the show. The bubbles pop fruitily on my tongue, but I don't want to drink. I lift one leg onto the bed and unfasten my suspenders, feeling as if we are in an old James Bond movie. He looks the part, and I feel it, sliding the silk down my leg, draping the stocking over the edge of the silk coverlet. Then the other leg, giving him the stocking so he can enjoy my fragrance while I remove the suspender belt. Kneeling up on the bed, between his legs, my hand rests naturally on the ridge in his dark purple cashmere trousers. It leaps into my hand and he gives me that dazzling smile.

'May I?' I ask.

'Oh, please do,' he says, and smiles, 'but I think I'd

better put this down first.' He gives me his champagne to put on the table. As I do so he grabs me and flings me down on the bed, causing me to shriek. He's tickling me with his hair, on the stomach, across the legs, and what started out as a seduction scene turns into a full-on rumple. We tumble on the bed, trying to outdo each other, until he slithers off onto the floor. Surprised, his head pops up and he comes for me, growling like a young lion. I dodge him and we end up chasing each other around the suite. Finally, breathless and laughing, I allow him to catch me and pin me to the bed again, sinking his teeth into my neck. The gentle bite turns into a kiss, and all at once he is passionate again, hungry for me, as if his need has been stoked even more by our recent play. I end up on top of him, scattering little biting kisses all over his body, moving down, unzipping his trousers and easing them away to the floor. By now he's churning his hips, suddenly desperate for the heat of my mouth. Dark cotton jockeys, as soft as cotton wool and distended by his arousal, are dispensed with and I can give him the pleasure he is crying out for.

'Oh fuck!' he cries out as he feels the heat surrounding him. I pull away, not wanting him to lose control too soon. He pulls me up so I can sit astride him. I feel dizzy as he eases inside me, this man, this icon I have admired on many occasions, now rocking me to the core with his heat. We start slow, smiling into each other's eyes, mutual understanding uniting us as much as our bodies are now joined. Slowly our expressions change as pure lust takes over, and our bodies pick up the tempo, rhythmically, finding the beat and sticking to it until our combined song of joy fills the whole room.

I collapse into his arms, my body gleaming with exertion. He cuddles up behind me, legs wrapped around mine, then traces down my spine with his finger.

'Don't think you're going to sleep. I haven't even started on you yet.'

BLACK LACE BOOKS

The world's leading imprint of erotic fiction for women

'They're written especially for women, so will hit the right buttons' *Maxim*

'Black Lace books create cult heroines' *Observer Life* magazine

If you enjoyed Abi's fantasies, you'll love ***The Black Lace Book of Women's Sexual Fantasies***

ISBN 0 352 33793 1 | **£6.99**

'Exhilarating and heart-warming ... a celebration of the glorious uncertainty of sex' *Daily Telegraph*

BLACK LACE

Black Lace publishes two titles every month and has a huge catalogue of arousing erotic novels and collections of short stories – available from all good bookshops or the website: **www.blacklace-books.co.uk** or **amazon.co.uk**